PRAISE FOR THE INSPECTOR DAVID GRAHAM MYSTERY SERIES

"I'm in love with him and his colleagues."

"A terrific mystery."

"This newest is like seeing old friends again and catching up on the latest news."

"These books certainly have the potential to become a PBS series with the likeable character of Inspector Graham and his fellow officers."

"Delightful writing that keeps moving, never a dull moment."

"I know I have a winner of a book when I toss and turn at night worrying about how the characters are doing."

"Love it and love the author."

"Refreshingly unique and so well written."

"Solid proof that a book can rely on good storytelling and good writing without needing blood or sex."

"This series just gets better and better."

"DI Graham is wonderful and his old school way of doing things, charming."

"Great character development."

“Super in all respects.”
“Please write more!”

THE CASE OF THE HIDDEN FLAME

ALSO BY ALISON GOLDEN

The Case of the Screaming Beauty (Prequel)

The Case of the Fallen Hero

The Case of the Broken Doll

The Case of the Missing Letter

The Case of the Pretty Lady

THE CASE OF THE HIDDEN FLAME

ALISON GOLDEN

GRACE DAGNALL

The characters and events portrayed in this book are fictitious. Any similarity to real persons, living or dead is coincidental and not intended by the author.

Published by Mesa Verde Publishing
P.O. Box 1002
San Carlos, CA 94070

Edited by
Marjorie Kramer

To Barb and Vikk,
Your advice and support mean more than you will ever know.

To get your free copy of *The Case of the Screaming Beauty,* the prequel to the Inspector David Graham series, plus two more books, updates about new releases, exclusive promotions, and other insider information, sign up for Alison's mailing list at:

https://www.alisongolden.com/graham

CHAPTER ONE

CONSTABLE JIM ROACH made quite sure that he wasn't being watched and then took a long moment to assess his appearance in the mirror. There would be only one chance, he knew, to make a first impression, and he was determined to single himself out as a man of both neatness and integrity; someone to be entrusted with the most challenging, perhaps even the most *dangerous* investigations. The new boss could well be his long-awaited passport to promotion. He might – the thought made his breath catch in his throat – *even* get to see a dead body for the first time. That was certainly worth a minute's close attentiveness to ensure that his tie was straight, his uniform spotless, jacket buttons gleaming, and his hair neatly in place under his blue constable's cap.

There. Perfect. He grinned conspiratorially at the face in the mirror and returned to the tiny police station's reception desk, where he busied himself with a quite unusual energy. "Shipshape and Bristol fashion," he muttered as he straightened the lobby chairs and then belatedly flipped over the calendar of fetching Jersey shoreline postcards from August to September. Behind the desk, there was a smattering of filing waiting for him, put off repeatedly for weeks, but accomplished in about six minutes, once he put his mind to it. The perennially available deck of cards was slid into a desk drawer. "No solitaire this shift, Constable Roach," he admonished himself. "The new boss wouldn't like it."

Familiar footsteps could be heard strolling into the reception area from the small hallway beyond, where the "new boss" would have his office. These were followed by an even more familiar voice, its Cockney accent robustly unchanged despite six years in Jersey.

"Bloody hell, Jim." The man stopped and stared. "Are we trying to win a contest or something?"

"What's that, mate?" Roach asked from behind the flip-top reception desk.

"I've never seen the place so tidy before," he explained. "Expecting company, are we?"

Barry "Bazza" Barnwell loved nothing more than needling his younger colleague, especially when Roach let slip his desire to get ahead in the Constabulary. Barnwell was older than Roach but he was as content as could be to remain what he called a "beat cop," while Roach had dreams of a sergeant's stripes and then much more. Scotland Yard. Detective Inspector. Chasing down terrorists and drug runners and murderers. *That* was where the action was. Gorey, pleasantly unchallenging as Barnwell found it, was merely a stepping stone for Constable Roach.

"It never hurts to put your best foot forward," Roach explained, continuing to tidy stacks of paper behind the desk.

"What do you think, eh?" Barnwell asked, leaning on the desk. "Once Mister High And Mighty arrives, you'll be immediately seconded to the bloody SAS or something?" he joked. "'Our man in Tangiers' within a month, is it?"

"Bazza," Roach replied wearily, polishing the much abused desk top with a yellow duster. "You may be happy on this little island, but I've got aspirations."

"Have you, by God?" Barnwell chuckled. "Well, I'd see a doctor if I were you, mate. Sounds painful. Not to mention a likely danger to yourself and others."

Roach ignored him, but there was little else to occupy them during this relaxed, summertime midmorning. Besides, Barnwell was having too much fun.

"I don't know if you'd be cut out for armed police or the riot squad, you know," he was chattering. "Chap like you? What is it now, a whole, great big, overwhelming *five* arrests... And three of those for tax evasion?"

This got Roach's goat. "There was that plonker on the beach who was trying to do things to that girl. Remember that, eh? Saved her *honor*, I did."

Barnwell doubled up laughing at the memory. "Oh yeah, first-rate police work, that was. She was only *there* because he'd already paid her a hundred quid, you wazzack. And *he* was only *trying*," Barnwell added, between convulsions of mirth, "because he'd had a skin full at the Lamb and Flag and could barely even..."

Saved by the phone. It was an old-fashioned ring – Roach had insisted – not one of those annoying, half-hearted ones that went *beep-beep* but a proper *telephone*.

"Gorey Police, Constable Roach speaking," he said, ignoring Barnwell's descent toward the reception room floor in a fit of his own giggles. "Yes, sir," Roach said crisply. "Understood, sir. We look forward to meeting you then, sir." He replaced the receiver.

"You forgot the 'three bags full, sir,'" Barnwell offered.

"Get yourself together, mate," Roach announced purposefully. "Our new overlord approaches."

"Who?" Barnwell asked, straightening his tie and biting off the remnants of his laughter.

"The new DI, you unmentionable so-and-so. And if you show me up, so help me..."

Roach became a whirlwind once more, carefully adjusting the time on the big wall clock in the reception area, one which looked as though it had done a century's steady labor in a train station waiting room. Then, to Barnwell's endless amusement, he watered the plants, including the incongruous but pleasingly bushy shrub in the corner, and trundled through to the back offices.

"Mind the fort, Constable Barnwell," he requested formally.

The hallway led to the DI's new office, hastily refurbished, which Roach already knew was in "shipshape," and a second office that was occupied by Sergeant Janice Harding. Janice was their immediate superior but given the regular antics of the two constables, she often felt as much like a nanny or a middle school dinner lady.

"Sarge, he's on his way from the airport in a cab," Roach announced.

"I heard the phone five minutes ago, Roach," she complained, standing suddenly. "It took you that long to tell me?"

Normally immune to any kind of fluster, it was both unique and amusing to see Janice sent into such a tizzy over this new arrival. Roach suspected that her interest was less in the possibility of career advancement and more in the new DI's reputation as a good-looking, old-fashioned charmer. There hadn't been a lot of luck with the men lately, Janice would concede, a point of particular concern given Jersey's limited supply of eligible bachelors. And, with Harding rapidly approaching her 'Big Three-Oh,' it was high time for that to change.

Janice brushed down her skirt, and ignoring Roach's looming presence in her doorway, tidied her hair in the mirror.

"Well, Roach? Is thc reception area looking..."

"Shipshape and Bristol fashion," Constable Roach reported proudly. "And his office is just how he asked for it."

"And what about Constable Barnwell?" she asked. She leaned close and whispered, "He hasn't been drinking, has he?"

"Not that I can tell," Jim whispered back.

"Good. We could all do without dealing with that nonsense, today of all days."

She shooed Roach out of the way and carried out her own inspection of their small police station. Roach shrugged as she found a number of things to improve – straightening the framed map of Jersey on the main wall and the two portraits of previous police chiefs – and then he went to find Barnwell in the station's equipment room.

"Remember what I said," Roach called out with all seriousness. "Professionalism and respect. You hear?"

"Loud and clear, future Chief Constable Roach," Barnwell quipped, hanging spare uniforms up in a neat line. "I'll make sure there's no getting off on the wrong foot."

Roach eyed him uncertainly. "You really want to be in here when he arrives or behind your desk where you belong?"

As luck would have it, Roach was answering a phone call from a member of the public when the new DI walked in, a black suitcase in each hand and dressed in a smart, grey suit. It was a relief not to have to *look* busy as he noted down the details of a stolen bicycle, lifted during the night from a back garden shed a few miles away. Sergeant Harding handled the introductions.

"Detective Inspector Graham, I'm so pleased to meet you and to welcome you to Gorey," she smiled. "I hope your flight was smooth?"

Graham set down the suitcases with a sigh of relief and smiled back, extending his hand. "Very smooth, thank you, Sergeant."

"Oh, you can call me Janice," she said, five times more flirtatiously than she had planned and ten times more than Graham would have preferred.

"And this must be Constable Roach?" he asked, approaching the desk with his hand out, just as the tall, red-headed man was finishing the call.

"Pleasure to meet you, sir," Roach said, just as he'd practiced.

"Anything interesting?" Graham said, glancing at the phone.

"Stolen bike, out near the golf course. Not unusual for this time of year. I'll head over there in a moment and take a statement," Roach said.

The station's only other permanent appointment appeared and was introduced by Harding. Roach watched the new boss' demeanor as he took in the burly six-foot frame of Constable Barnwell with a curious interest. Was he looking for signs of drink? Roach wondered if that particular piece of intelligence had filtered up to London or not. If so, what did the top brass know about *him*? Was Graham here to ensure that a potential high-flyer was given every chance to prove himself? A golden future offered itself to Roach in those heady moments. Then it was back to earth.

"I'll take that statement," Janice told him rather curtly.

"I can do it once I've dropped off DI Graham at the White House Inn."

There would be, Roach saw at once, absolutely no discussion on this point. Fifteen minutes alone in a car with their new arrival was apparently well worth the tedious grunt work of noting down this rather routine complaint.

"Very good, Sarge," Roach replied. "You'll enjoy the White House, Detective Inspector. Nice place." He thought on for a second. "Roomy."

"I'm sure I will," David Graham told him, refusing a polite offer of help with his suitcases. He slid them into the trunk of Harding's blue-and-white police sedan and still fawning over him like an adolescent, the Sergeant drove him along the coastal road toward Gorey itself.

"You've arrived in just the *best* part of the year," Harding enthused. "The tourists can be a nightmare, but there never seems to be more than we can cope with," she said. "It will make a big change from London."

Graham was soaking up the scenery; the small, neat houses by the road, the farms with walking, fluffy clouds that must have been sheep, the pleasant mix of sultry summer warmth and upbeat, fun-loving energy that Jersey had become famous for. As they approached the cliffs on which the seaside resort of Gorey perched, the green fields gave way to sparkling blue ocean and the marina beyond, festooned with pleasure craft of all sizes.

"Beautiful," Graham found himself saying. "Not a lot like London, you're right there, Sergeant Harding."

Tourists were gathered in little knots, eating ice cream, deciding where to have a late lunch, sometimes popping into one of the local shops for supplies.

"The White House Inn is up on the hill there," Harding pointed. It was an imposing, solid building, aptly named. Its paintwork shone brilliantly in the early afternoon sunshine. It reminded Graham of a rural French chateau, uprooted and then plonked on this towering cliff, providing perhaps the most spectacular and restful views on the island.

"A little B&B would have done the trick, you know," Graham admitted.

"Oh, nonsense," Harding said, waving him away. "We wanted you to feel welcome here. I'd be happy to help find you somewhere more permanent, but I'm sure you'll be comfortable at the White House for the time being. The tea room has the best cakes on Jersey and..."

"There's a tea room?" Graham interrupted, his curiosity instantly piqued.

"Yes, indeed. They have all those "frou-frou" types of teas, if you like that kind of thing." Harding chuckled. "Why?"

"Oh, nothing," he replied, biting down his enthusiasm. "Just good to know, " he added with a slight smile.

The lobby boded well, high-ceilinged and tastefully decorated with flowered wallpaper, statues and a venerable grandfather clock which thundered out the two o'clock chime just as he was checking in.

"Ah yes, Detective Inspector Graham," the clerk said, finding him quickly on the reception desk's tablet. "I've put you in one of our nicest rooms, overlooking the marina."

"Splendid," Graham said. "Is the hotel busy at the moment?"

His black hair swept back by copious gel, the clerk reminded Graham of an extra from a pulp novel set during the Roaring Twenties. All that was missing was the pencil mustache and a quick blast of the Charleston.

"Almost full, I'm glad to say. Mostly long-termers," he said, and then explained further when he saw Graham's quizzical expression. "Retirees, sir, people who prefer to live a more active lifestyle rather than checking into one of the retirement homes here on the island. There's plenty to do," he said, handing Graham a brochure from behind the desk. "Sailing, swimming, windsurfing, fishing.... Enough to keep anyone out of trouble," he winked.

"Trouble?" Graham said, quickly.

"Just my little joke, sir," he smiled. "Here's hoping you'll have a quiet stay in Jersey. We're a pretty unspectacular bunch, I'm glad to say."

"Splendid," Graham replied again, rather automatically, as he scanned the brochure. "I'll unpack and then maybe try a pot of one of your famous teas."

"Best on the island, sir," he said proudly, handing Graham his key. "I do hope you enjoy your stay." He tapped the tablet a few times and scuttled over to welcome a group of tired-looking Germans who were sweating profusely with the weight of three truly gigantic suitcases.

A well-traveled and rather sophisticated man despite his rustic Yorkshire roots, Graham was not easily impressed by hotel rooms, having seen many. However, his room at the White House Inn was large with a comfortable bed, and boasted a view of the ocean, the marina, and Gorey beach that was simply breathtaking. He opened the windows wide and took three long, deep breaths of cleansing sea air.

"Entirely adequate," he mused to himself before heading down to the tea room in the hopes of a delicate Assam or Darjeeling. "Yes, indeed. This will do nicely."

Nearly one hundred feet below, a tall figure of purposeful – one would almost say *military* – bearing was striding down the beach on his afternoon walk. Colonel Graves, a man whose retention of his army title was not simply an affectation but rather also a statement of his values, brought down his tall cane into the sand with a mechanical precision that in its very rhythm pleased him greatly. It was important to keep one's own traditions, he'd always felt. Especially during retirement, when one was apt, in the absence of care and discipline, to become addled and flabby, two things which were anathema to the sixty-year-old ex-officer.

In an open-collared, eggshell-blue shirt and pressed khaki shorts, he was every inch the self-exiled retiree, enjoying hard-earned sunshine and spending hard-earned savings. For him, a lifetime of service had left little time for family or even courting. There had been women, of course, but none who had wanted to stick by the kind of chap who would jet off to war every few years, returning each time a little more cynical, a little less certain of his belief in the fundamental goodness of humanity, each time somehow *older* than before. He had survived the Argentine fighter bombers strafing his ship in the Falklands, the best efforts of Saddam Hussein's Republican Guard, and six months among the Taliban of Helmand before something in him had simply said *stop*. And so, to Jersey, where he busied himself keeping in shape, visiting the old German fortifications from World War II, and keeping an eye out for Miss Right.

Or, he chuckled – hang it all, we only live once – *Mrs*. Right, for that matter.

It was just this attentiveness, which usually let not a detail pass by, which brought him to a discovery both heartbreaking and, even for a military man, unbearably gruesome.

Just where the beach met the sea wall, the sand swelled

up into a mini dune, perhaps four feet high, studded with tufts of grass and a discarded soda bottle, Graves noted with distaste. But then there was something else, and it attracted his eye because it absolutely *did not belong*.

It was a dainty, pale, human hand.

"Well, what in the blazes...?" he muttered darkly.

His first thought, given the location, was that this might be someone washed onto the beach from the ocean. An unfortunate migrant, perhaps, dead from exposure and then deposited here at high tide. This would hardly be his first encounter with a corpse, but a quiet beach on this idyllic little island was the last place he'd expect to see one. He frowned and slowly approached the small rise of the dune, peering at the hand as if it might transform into something innocuous, and this strange moment might then be discarded as no more than a reason to visit the eye doctor.

He knelt by the dune and carefully smoothed away a little of the sand that covered what was clearly the almost translucent skin of an inanimate forearm. At once, the Colonel knew that this was no washed-up asylum seeker. Nor was this some prank, the kids burying their mother in the sand and then forgetting about her as ice cream and soda beckoned.

There was a silver bracelet, rather expensive, which shone brightly now in the sun. And it was instantly familiar.

"Oh, no," Graves shuddered. "Oh, good *heavens*, no..."

"Gorey Police Station, Constable Barnwell speaking." Barnwell's bright and cheerful manner contrasted markedly with the tone of this caller, only the third of the day. It was the sound of a man still struggling to bring his emotions under control despite decades of practice.

"Yes, I'm... erm... This is Colonel George Graves, and I'm calling from the beach at Gorey, just opposite the pier and about ten yards west of the stone stairs that lead down from the Inn," he said. Barnwell, who was struck by the Colonel's precision, began making notes at once. "Yes, sir?"

The Colonel took a breath. "There's... Well, a *body* here."

Barnwell's eyebrows shot up. He gesticulated toward the office where Roach was filling out a report.

"*Get in here*!" he whispered loudly.

"I see, sir," he said, bringing his most professional and sober tone. "Have you checked for signs of life?"

"Yes, and I'm afraid there are none," Graves said soberly. "No pulse. And... Well, I believe I may *know* her, you see."

The bushy black eyebrows were aloft once again. Just for a second, Barnwell felt that he might be about to hear a man confess to a murder.

"Are you able to identify the deceased, sir?"

Graves cleared his throat and bit back the urge to unleash some of the emotion he was feeling. It wasn't *fair*. They'd met only a few months earlier, just after Graves arrived on Jersey to begin a long hoped-for retirement of sand and sun and...

"I believe it's Dr. Sylvia Norquist. She's a resident at the White House Inn. I have..." he began, fighting back his first tears in many years, "I have no idea how she came to be here."

No confession, then, Barnwell noted with a slump of his shoulders.

"Well, sir. You've done the right thing. And I'm sorry

for your trouble. As it happens," he said, one hand aloft and circling in his continuing efforts to get Roach's attention, "our new Detective Inspector has just checked into the White House. I'll let him know what's happened and ask him to join you immediately."

"Do I need to do anything?" Graves wanted to know. "Call her family?"

"We should wait until there's a formal identification. Would you simply stay where you are for the moment? Detective Inspector Graham will be with you shortly."

Graves said that he would before ending the call.

He squatted uncomfortably by the sand dune, part of him needing to hold the small, ash-white hand, another repelled by it, and yet another simply stunned at the continued, harsh *unreasonableness* of the world.

"Oh, my darling," he said softly, a single tear finally rolling down his face. "My darling girl. Whatever happened?"

DI David Graham found Graves sitting by the dune. Graves looked shattered, ashen and old beyond his years.

"Colonel Graves?"

He stood and extended a hand, more by habit than any impulse to be friendly. "At your service."

"I'm truly sorry, sir. And I understand that you knew her?" It was always troublesome, Graham found, to select the most appropriate tense in these situations. Using the past tended to reinforce the unrelenting reality of the loss, but the present seemed strange, uncomprehending, a form of denial.

"Quite well. We were..." It took all of the military man's

trained self-control to keep his composure. "I was going to ask her to marry me, you see." His gaze became distant, his jaw muscles tensing rhythmically as he began to contend with the pain of his own grief, with the lost promise of happiness so brutally snatched from him.

Graham brought out his notebook – he was still an old-school pen and paper type – and began making notes. "And when did you last see her?"

Graves thought for a moment. "We had dinner two nights ago. At the Marina. She was in great spirits. Full of life," he said, with great pain. "We are both residents at the White House Inn," he explained further.

"But you hadn't proposed yet?" Graham asked as sensitively as he could.

"No," Graves said, shaking his head sadly. "Should have taken my chance, eh, Detective?" He felt the need to sit down again, his legs unsteady and balance betraying him. "Oh, *God*, the poor girl..."

Graham brought out his phone, turning to mask his words amid the waves of the low tide.

"Barnwell? Yes, I'm here with Colonel Graves. I need an ambulance – discreetly, Barnwell, let's not make a fuss if we can help it... and the pathologist.... Good man. Quick as you can. And send Harding to secure a room at the White House Inn... Sylvia Norquist."

Graham took a moment to spell the name. He turned to see Graves staring inconsolably at the sand dune then spoke into the phone once again.

"That's it for now, Barnwell."

Two volunteer Community Support Officers in their reflective yellow tunics kept back a small crowd as the pathologist, Dr. Marcus Tomlinson, and his assistant delicately brushed sufficient sand from the body to carry out their initial investigations. Tomlinson was a 40-year veteran, thorough and perceptive, and little escaped him. He took Graham to the shoreline so that they could speak without being overheard.

"The time of death will be difficult to ascertain. The sand, sea, and salty air all combine to mess with the state of the body." Tomlinson was apologetic.

"Can you give me a clue?" Graham retorted.

"My best guess is sometime in the last eighteen hours. I can't be more accurate than that, I'm afraid." Tomlinson reported.

"Hmm," Graham was surprised. "So she could have ended up here in the middle of the night, or she may have keeled over at midday on a busy beach?" he said, thinking out loud.

"Admittedly," Tomlinson added, "on one of its quietest stretches." They both glanced around and noted the secluded nature of the spot, beneath the steps but away from the broader, most popular stretch of sand. "I'll know more once we complete toxicology screens," Tomlinson told him, "but for the moment we can't rule out foul play."

"Oh?" Graham said, witnessing the complexity of this case ballooning before his eyes.

"She's in her fifties, and according to the Colonel, in robust health apart from needing a double hip replacement. Although you hear the uninitiated say it often enough," Tomlinson warned, "people generally don't simply keel over and die. After four decades in this business, I've become a firm believer in cause and effect. Plus she was buried. It's windy today but not so much that it would have whipped up the sand to that extent."

"So you think," Graham asked, his voice deliberately low despite the waves crashing a few feet away, "she was murdered?"

Tomlinson shrugged. "Like I say, no way of knowing until the tox report is in." He referred to his own notebook, shrugged, and closed it. "Standing here, right now, I'd bet fifty guineas and dinner at the Bangkok Palace that Dr. Norquist met her end neither by her own hand nor by natural causes."

DI Graham cursed colorfully under his breath. "You know I've been here five minutes, right?" he mused aloud.

"And you know we haven't had a murder here since the Newall Brothers axed their parents for their inheritance money, back when you were in college?" the older man replied. He gave Graham a comradely pat on the back. "Well, DI Graham, welcome to the Bailiwick of Jersey."

CHAPTER TWO

MRS. MARJORIE TAYLOR, the matronly owner of the White House Inn, was caught between moments of great anxiety, genuine grief, and her wish to be as useful to the police as possible. She simply couldn't believe that a nice lady like Sylvia – a respected oncologist and a pillar of their close-knit community – could have been taken from them so suddenly. So *terribly*. Why, she had eaten lunch just a couple of hours ago! But being the good citizen and innkeeper that she was, Mrs. Taylor worked to find a balance between helping the police and carrying out much-needed rumor control, lest her guests suddenly decide to check out *en masse* in a fit of panic and ruin the Inn's precious summer.

"We'll aim to cause as little disruption as possible," DI Graham informed her during a short meeting in her office just off the hotel's lobby. "But it's important that no one except the police enters her room. We can do without 'Police Caution' tape everywhere," he assured her, "but we must be thorough."

"I appreciate your discretion," Marjorie said. "This is just so... *awful*."

It was the same word everyone seemed to use on first learning the sad news. "Too *awful*," one said. "Simply *awful*," commented another. The only person who had said no such thing was Constable Roach, who saw not just a silver lining to this cloud, but also that the cloud itself was laden with gold. Career-making gold, at that.

Sylvia's was a corner room on the third floor, to Marjorie Taylor's relief, so that the police could gather evidence without disturbing the rest of the hotel. Still, the sight of blue uniforms did cause some flutters, and the spreading news brought a tense, worried atmosphere to the place. Marjorie told the tea room staff to waive everyone's checks for the rest of the day and the bar staff to do the same in the evening. It was the least she could do, the experienced hotelier reasoned to herself.

Dr. Norquist's room was neat almost to the point of obsession.

"No signs of a struggle," concluded Constable Roach.

He was elbowed aside by Sergeant Harding, who led DI Graham into the room.

"Thanks, Sherlock," she whispered with heavy sarcasm. "Once you're finished here, you can get back to finding Jack the Ripper. For the moment, just watch the stairs, like I told you to. And keep Mrs. Taylor company. She's a bit jittery with all that's going on."

"Yes, ma'am. No one's to come up without your say-so," he replied crisply, hiding his hurt at the jibe. *When I release my tell-all book in a few years' time and become a crime-fighting media celebrity, you'll rue the day....*

"So she was here at lunchtime," Graham mused, looking about the room.

"Would seem like it, sir," Harding responded.

"And she ordered the fish," observed Graham. "Mostly uneaten, too." Atop the room's oak dresser was a gleaming, silver tray with a single plate, a small vase with a bright daisy, and silverware. He smelled the food. "Chili, ginger... But no indication that the fish was off," he concluded.

"I mean," Harding began, poking at the fish with Sylvia's fork, "if the fish had been rotten enough to poison someone, wouldn't it have been obvious as she was eating it?"

"Yes, we can rule that out," Graham told her, writing the details in his notebook. "Mrs. Taylor?" he called out. "Do you know who brought Dr. Norquist's lunch today?"

The rotund lady appeared around the corner, along with the intensely curious Constable Roach.

"That would have been Marcella," she replied. "Lovely girl," she said, turning to Harding. "From Lisbon. She sets the tray outside the door and knocks. That's always been our policy."

Graham asked, "So she wouldn't have heard anything through the door?"

"We are not in the habit," Marjorie replied a little testily, "of listening at our residents' doors, Inspector. Sylvia had a male friend, and one never knows what one might overhear. My guests are often very private people," she said, proud of the service she provided but equally keen to help. "You know, I could think all day and all next year, and I wouldn't know a single soul who might want to hurt that dear lady."

Graham finished his notes and slid the book back into his jacket pocket. "Well, I suspect *someone* did, Mrs. Taylor," Graham said soberly. "And I'm afraid," he added with a strange frown, "that they're right under our noses."

Sitting resolutely upright, staring out to sea from his table by the window, Colonel Graves ignored the pot of tea laid out for him by the concerned and sympathetic staff. As Graham approached, Graves made to stand, but the detective waved him to his seat.

"At ease, Colonel," Graham said, but regretted the quip. This wasn't the moment for levity. At least, Graham could see, the Colonel seemed to have gathered himself a little since their encounter on the beach, but both men knew that Graves would be carrying the emotional weight of his terrible discovery for the rest of his life.

"Have you found anything new, Detective?" Graves asked. He still looked ashen and careworn, but his straight back and clipped diction gave him a stoical air, like that of a man forced to deal with the worst kind of news but doing so with grace and determination.

One of the tea room's more experienced waitresses, the aforementioned Marcella from Portugal approached with her notepad, and Graham couldn't help ordering a pot of Fujian Jasmine.

"Nothing concrete," he admitted. "At this stage, it's more a case of eliminating lines of inquiry," Graham explained. "We know that Sylvia was not poisoned by her lunch, but that's about all so far."

"Poison?" Graves spoke the word in a hushed, stunned tone. "So this was deliberate?"

Treading carefully, Graham said, "We mustn't jump to conclusions, certainly not as early as this." Once Marcella returned, he poured his own tea with an almost ritualistic fluency of movement. "I'm waiting to hear back from the pathologist. I'm sorry," he said, meeting the older man's gaze. "This must be just awful."

Colonel Graves sighed. "Were you in the service, Detective?" Graham shook his head. "I've seen things so dreadful I've sworn never to speak of them to anyone. Things happen," he said, steepling his hands on the table top, "to your friends, to your enemies, that humans should never do to another. But," he said, straightening his back once more, "that's war. One does what is necessary. Sylvia was not at war, Detective. She never hurt a soul. It is *that* which bothers me the most."

Graham noted the word – *bothers*. It wasn't what the Colonel meant, but it befit the bearing of a man trained in self-control, well-practiced in keeping hidden that which should not become public. Graham felt a real sympathy for him, which was why he resented the necessity of eliminating Graves himself from the inquiry.

"Colonel, I'm sorry to ask this, but..."

"Where was I at lunchtime today?" he said.

"Like I say, I'm sorry..."

"You're following procedure, Detective. I'd have been surprised if you hadn't asked me. Not a little disappointed, too."

"Really?" Graham asked, lifting the teacup sufficiently to enjoy the floral waft of Jasmine.

"Sylvia was to be my wife," Graves said solemnly. "At least, if she had accepted my proposal. And I expected her to, you know." He was nostalgic once again. "I'm not the finest catch in the ocean, I'm sure of that... But we would have been *happy* together. That's all any of us wants, isn't it?"

Graham felt reassured by this more philosophical side to the Colonel but was aware that Graves had yet to actually answer his question. "So, at lunchtime?" he said. "Just for my notes."

"I was on the phone to my real estate broker in London for about an hour, all told. Bloody tedious stuff but had to be done. I'm trying to make a few quid over in the States with quick house renovations in desirable areas. Buy them, do them up, sell them on, you know. Here," he said, handing Graham his cell phone. "You can check the call history. No warrant required," he added.

"That won't be necessary," Graham said, resolved that he was not in the company of a killer. There had been a flash of concern just after Graves had admitted being of a mind to propose to Sylvia. The Colonel would hardly have been the first man to react badly to a refusal, but there was nothing in his behavior to suggest that he was anything other than sadly and unfortunately bereaved.

"She wanted to come on my afternoon strolls," Graves continued. "I always head down the beach for a mile or two after lunch. But she suffered terribly with her hips."

Graham was writing once more. "Was it very serious?" he asked.

"Serious enough that she could barely have gone down the steps to the beach unaided," he said. "Stairs were tremendously painful for her. Without the elevator, she'd have been asking to be moved to the ground floor of the Inn," he explained.

Graham began wondering at once: How on earth did she manage the stairs down to the beach, except in the company of someone? Perhaps the murderer? And why would she submit to going on such a painful walk? He made another note and then slid the book home in his jacket.

"Well, Colonel. If you think of anything which might

help us, please do get in touch." Graham finished his cup and rose, extending his hand.

Graves did the same, his grip firm despite slightly unsteady legs. "I will. Might I..." he began, and then leaned close. "You'll let me know, won't you? If you find who did this?"

"Of course," Graham said, sensing that in doing so he might condemn the murderer to suffer a visitation from a distressed but lethal Graves. "You'll be the first to know," he lied.

The Inn's lobby was mercifully clear of concerned guests, leaving Mrs. Taylor to continue telling Sergeant Harding and Constable Barnwell every last detail she could think of regarding her guests and their relationships with Sylvia Norquist. The police officers were developing a picture of a quiet but personable lady who was both respected and admired. Some of the other guests had reported seeing Sylvia and Colonel Graves dining together some evenings, or taking a leisurely afternoon tea in the hotel. The couple were thought to be simply adorable.

Mrs. Taylor put it as only she could. "Two lonely people, providing comfort and company for each other in their later years. It was enough to warm the heart."

Alongside the tales of blossoming romance, though, were the very beginnings of what Detective Graham knew might become *leads*. He was in desperate need of information that might bring this case out of what was the least welcome category of deaths for a detective; victims who were found alone, with little forensic evidence, no witnesses, and no immediate suspects or motives. Graham just *hated* those, but he turned the emotion into a determination to gather more evidence, interview more people, and pester the lab until they came up with something more concrete than Tomlinson's educated guesswork.

"Tell me about the Pilkingtons," he said, reading the name from Sergeant Harding's list of those to be interviewed. "It says here that they knew Sylvia."

"Oh yes," Mrs. Taylor said at once. She was proving to be quite the store of gossip, which made her an ideal source of information in a case like this. "They've been friends for a long time. I could be wrong," she said cautiously, "but I believe Mr. Pilkington was under Dr. Norquist for some time."

Janice Harding's artless, barely constrained guffaw caused a rapid re-phrasing from Mrs. Taylor. "I mean, he was her *patient*," she clarified, red-faced. "Cancer, I think." She swatted at Janice's uniformed arm in chuckling rebuke.

Graham paid the bawdy comedy no mind and pressed on. "I'd like to speak with them both. Are they here at the moment?"

The Pilkingtons were an affluent, sophisticated couple, Graham could see at once. Their room was as neat as Sylvia's had been, but their belongings spoke of class; a hand-made pashmina scarf, a Gucci purse, and Mr. Pilkington stood in an immaculate Savile Row suit.

"Mr. and Mrs. Pilkington, I'm sorry to disturb you. But I'm sure you've heard..." The couple waved Graham and Sergeant Harding into the room. They took a corner armchair and the desk's leather-bound seat.

The gaunt, long-faced Pilkington said nothing, seemingly content to let his wife do the talking. "Sylvia was our doctor, back in London," Mrs. Pilkington offered. She sat on the edge of the bed, her Gucci bag clasped tightly, as though one of these new arrivals might try to make off with it. "She cured Nigel's cancer. Amazing doctor," she said, rather gushingly, as one might describe a new hairdresser whom you simply *had* to try.

"Were you aware," Harding asked, "that she was here on Jersey? You know, before you arrived here?"

Anne Pilkington was shaking her head, but before she could speak, it was Nigel's voice they heard, low and sad. "I was. Dr. Norquist is the reason I encouraged Anne to move here for the summer. I've been seeing her, you see."

Mrs. Pilkington twisted suddenly to face her husband. "Nigel? Why didn't you... I mean... How could you..."

Entirely unwilling to bear witness to an impromptu domestic hissy-fit, Graham interrupted. "When, Mr. Pilkington?"

"The first time was about six weeks ago," he said, a little more confident now, as though the presence of police officers might protect him from his wife's sudden and growing anger. "I met her in the village," he smiled thinly, before catching Anne's furious expression and wilting slightly.

"And you spent some time together?" Sergeant Harding asked delicately. Her tone carried no insinuation, Graham was relieved to hear, but this did nothing to calm Mrs. Pilkington, whose assumptions of infidelity were as plain as the lettering on her Gucci bag.

"We caught up, as old friends do," he explained, his face innocent. Graham wondered quite why his wife had rushed to assumptions and anger, and concluded that, as in most long marriages, there were undercurrents that others could never know. Secrets that might never see the light of day, lest the delicate house of cards come crashing down. "I saw her on... what would it be," he searched his memory, "the end of last week. We had coffee in the village."

"You said you were going to the *post office* to send a card to Margaret after her dog died!" Anne Pilkington exclaimed in a furious roar. Graham judged her reaction commensurate with her husband having confessed to killing the dog himself during a deranged Satanic ritual, rather than anything as benign as having coffee with his old doctor. "Why?" she demanded, tears starting to fall.

As the couple confronted each other in a stony, accusatory silence, Sergeant Harding caught Graham's eye and mouthed, "*What the heck?*"

Graham shrugged with genuine confusion. *These older couples*, he mused to himself. His parents were the same. Forty-one years of marriage, and they could still get each other riled up over the simplest thing.

But this exchange between the long-married couple threatened to derail their interview and might limit how much they learned about Sylvia's comings and goings, and the people they knew. Graham stepped in.

"Mrs. Pilkington, we're trying to build a picture of Sylvia's habits and relationships. At the moment, her only romance seems to have been with Colonel Graves, and they were close to becoming engaged." He hoped this news might assuage Anne Pilkington's coursing anger.

"Seems to have been?" she demanded, almost shrieking at the detective.

"Anne, listen," Nigel said in the plaintive tone of a man entirely disinterested in a protracted argument with a hysterical wife. "I needed her advice. It's... Well, I should have told you months ago, but..."

Anne's expression changed as quickly as a cloud covers the sun. "Nigel? What is it, darling? *Tell* me."

Nigel glanced awkwardly at the two officers, and Graham was halfway to standing before Nigel spoke again.

"I was thinking of suicide. The cancer. It's back. And it's bad."

Jesus. Graham watched the two embrace and console one another for a truly awkward minute before it was clear they would learn nothing more until the couple gathered themselves.

"We'll be going," Harding said gently. "Thank you for your time, and... We're sorry for your troubles. Both of you."

Graham nodded in comradely approval, and they took their leave, closing the door very quietly behind them. "Conclusions, Sergeant Harding?" Graham asked as they headed down the hallway toward the stairs.

"Don't marry a crazy, suspicious person," she said.

"Very droll. Do you think Mrs. Pilkington was genuine? I mean," he said, pulling Harding aside at the top of the stairs, "was she learning of the renewed acquaintance between Sylvia and her husband for the first time?"

Harding shrugged. "It sounded pretty convincing to me, sir. If that was acting, it deserved an Oscar. Why do you ask?"

Graham's notebook was out once more. "Because if she already had her suspicions and murdered Sylvia to bring an end to her husband's affair..." He left the rest unspoken and made a string of notes in his distinctive, cursive handwriting, a legacy of strict schooling and a passion for neatness.

His pen only stopped when they spotted Marcella down the hallway.

"Whose room is this?" Graham asked her. The diminutive woman, as young as twenty, Graham guessed, was picking up a lunch tray from in front of the door.

"Alice," she said at first, but then corrected herself. "Miss Swift." Marcella was visibly uncomfortable to be suddenly questioned by the police. "I bring her lunch every day," she said, her Portuguese accent drawing out the vowel sound until the word was closer to 'launch'. "Is a problem?"

"No, no," Graham assured her. "Carry on as normal."

Marcella seemed grateful to be excused but more due to the challenges of communicating, Graham concluded, than any nefarious involvement in the day's events. He knocked on the door with three swift taps.

"Marcella?" came a voice from inside.

"No, it's the Jersey Police, Miss Swift. May we have a word?" Sergeant Harding said. She assumed that they might receive a warmer reception if Alice Swift heard a female voice at her door.

"The police?" she asked, blinking, as she opened the door. Then her tone softened, and her face fell. "Oh, I suppose you're here about that poor woman?"

"Yes, I'm afraid so," Graham told her.

"Terrible thing. Come in," Alice said, beckoning the pair inside. Her room was rather more austere than the Pilkington's, *though*, Graham mused to himself, *so is Harrods.* It was dominated by a wooden contraption which he took a moment to identify.

"You're a weaver," Graham finally said, admiring the work. "How wonderful. Is it a hobby or your profession?"

Alice returned to the wooden stool by her loom but turned to face the two officers. "A little of both, I'd say," Alice replied. Approaching forty, she was far from unattractive, Graham couldn't help noticing, but there was something stand-offish about her character which made him slightly suspicious. "I'm planning on opening my own shop in London."

"Wonderful!" Graham said again. Inwardly, he wondered at the economic sense of such a venture, but when someone is driven by a will to accomplish something...

"Have you found out anything more about Sylv-, I mean, the victim?" This question was to Sergeant Harding, who had stepped back to allow Graham to work his magic. It was one of the advantages of his natural charm, she was beginning to assume, that female witnesses might be more forthcoming.

"Well, the investigation has just begun," Harding told her. "We're just getting started interviewing people here at the Inn."

Alice brushed hair out of her eyes and regarded the detective. "Surely you can't believe that one of the guests did this," she said.

Something clicked in Graham's mind. "Did *what*?" he asked.

"I mean..." Alice began. "She was only in her fifties, wasn't she? Couldn't have been natural causes, though you never know, people do simply drop dead sometimes for no good reason."

Graham was glancing around the room, taking in the spools of material, the neatly lined-up pots of dye and paint on the mantle, the smaller threads carefully wrapped around templates the size of business cards and stored in a basket, ordered by hue.

He thought back to Tomlinson's comment on the beach. "Actually, that's hardly ever what happens," he said, almost to himself. Alice watched him become distant for a few moments, curious as to how the man's mind was working. Then, Graham remembered the lunch tray.

"Can I ask what you've eaten today, Miss Swift?"

Taken aback and squinting at the detective, Alice answered, "Well, I hardly think that has anything to do with it."

"Answer the question, if you would, Miss Swift." Harding's gentle nudge was sufficient.

"Coconut chicken and rice," she said. "The chef has been adding some light, Asian-themed lunches to the menu. It was very nice. Not too spicy."

Even before she'd finished her description, Graham was focusing on the tapestry which was in a half-completed state on Alice's loom. The bright azure blue of the ocean caught his eye first, then two racing sailboats, neck and neck, their sails billowing. On the shore beyond, onlookers waved cheerily under a sky dotted with wispy clouds.

"This really is terrific," he said.

Alice shone with pride. "It's going to be a wedding gift. Son of a friend. He's marrying a landlubber from Sevenoaks but swears he'll make a sailor of her."

"Very imaginative," Graham continued appreciatively, drawing a raised eyebrow from Harding. Utilizing one's charm to encourage a reluctant witness was one thing, but this was far closer to simple flirting. She felt a stab of jealousy. Alice was clearly smart and creative, probably well-traveled too, and what man would fail to be impressed by those gorgeous, carefree curls, and the way her flowing, hippy-dippy dress was stretched tight across her chest like a canvas on a frame, or indeed, the threads on her loom...

"Sergeant, I think we're done here," Graham told her. "Thank you for your time, Miss Swift."

The artist stood and shook Graham's hand, settling for a cute wave to Sergeant Harding. Janice faked a smile and tried to set aside the grumpy thoughts. *Try working for a living, sweetheart, rather than making pretty pictures of boats. A shop in London... Give me a break.*

Outside, Graham caught her moping expression. "A suspect?" he asked.

It wasn't what Harding had expected. "Why should she be?" They descended the stairs together. "She barely seemed to know Sylvia, and I can't see a motive there. Unless Sylvia insulted one of her stitch-pictures."

"Tapestries," Graham corrected her. "And she's got real talent."

They reached the lobby and Graham asked for the latest news from Barnwell. "A pair of them, by all accounts," Harding grumbled, *sotto voce*.

CHAPTER THREE

A DAPPER, ALMOST cheerful Dr. Tomlinson strode into the police station's reception area, slid a manila folder onto the desk in front of Constable Barnwell, and tapped it twice with his finger. "Tell your new boss," the elderly pathologist said proudly, "that he owes me dinner at the Bangkok Palace."

The toxicology screen had been returned in record time, partly at DI Graham's own urging, but mostly because Tomlinson was genuinely curious to know the truth. Murders were not exactly a dime a dozen on Jersey. In his whole time as pathologist here, he'd dealt with only five, and that record went back to the early 1980s. There had been suicides, of course, some of which had initially raised suspicions of foul play, but the evidence had quickly confirmed otherwise. In most cases, Tomlinson was forced to submit the sad, dreary ruling that another ambitious stockbroker had bitten off more than he could chew and decided to end his days in the harbor or in a luxury apartment in the company of a bottle of scotch and some pills. It was a lot more CSI-Jersey than CSI-*New* Jersey, all in all.

"Okay, then. Let's have it." Graham waved Tomlinson to a seat in his office, and the older man closed the door. The DI had returned to the station from the White House Inn to review what they'd discovered so far. He was enjoying the day's second pot of tea, its invigorating and slightly floral scents lending a welcome elegance to his bare and as-yet unimpressive office.

"Asphyxia," Tomlinson enunciated. "It's the only thing I'm certain of at the moment."

Graham turned the report to face him and scanned its conclusions. "Before she was buried in the sand, or after?"

"Before," Tomlinson confirmed. "No signs of sand in her airways. You'd have expected that," he explained, "even if she were unconscious when buried."

Unlike most police officers, or even members of the general public, Graham was aware that asphyxia was a *mode* of dying, not a *cause*. "So, what killed her?"

Tomlinson retrieved the report and took a seat, wincing as his old knees bent. "Well, it's relatively simple. It's all in the weight of the *lungs*, you see."

"Lungs?" Graham asked, reaching for his notebook.

"Heavy lungs indicate that the victim's heart went on beating for a time – perhaps as long as twenty minutes – after respiration ceased."

This was news to Graham. "That long?"

"Surprising, isn't it? How determinedly the human spirit clings to life, even when all hope is gone and brain functions are damned near ceased. But, Sylvia's lungs were no heavier than yours or mine, as we sit here."

Graham did the math. "So, her heart stopped at about the same time that she stopped breathing."

"Or even before," Tomlinson added.

"But why?"

"That's where you have me," the pathologist confessed. "Right now, I don't have a reason. Something caused her heart to stop, but otherwise it was perfectly healthy."

"So what do you think happened?" Graham asked, curious to learn if the older, more experienced man had a theory.

"My view hasn't changed from when I saw her on the beach. I'd bet my last penny and all the others, that Sylvia's death was no natural event. Like I said then, people rarely just keel over. Besides, if she quietly died of natural causes in her hotel room, who in God's name would find the body and then drag it down some stairs to bury it in the sand?"

"So, it's murder," Graham breathed. "You're certain?"

"As Christmas. Dinner is on you, Detective Inspector."

Graham nodded. He really wasn't sure if Tomlinson's findings were good news or bad. Part of him had been willing Sylvia Norquist's untimely demise to be the result of an odd manifestation of natural causes. The idea that there was a murderer lurking in the White House Inn was unsettling, especially given the paucity of apparent motives. At least, so far.

"What's your best guess at present?" he asked, deliberately pressing Tomlinson.

"A poison," he said at once. "Something which causes the body to shut down, the heart and respiration to stop. But I can't be sure. Could we ask the local doctors if they've prescribed anything which might cause an overdose? The kind of thing which wouldn't show up on a toxicology screen?"

"It's a long shot," Graham countered. "Most of that stuff is tied up in patient confidentiality. It could be weeks before we got a warrant to search any doctor's records, even if we could identify the prescribing physician. And there must be dozens, even somewhere as small as Jersey."

"There are twenty-nine," Tomlinson replied crisply. "I know most of them. I could put the word around, you know, see if anything comes up."

"Like what?" Graham asked, returning the folder.

"Oh, you know, a 'special request' by a patient who presents themselves in the doctor's office but without the appropriate symptoms, or one who seems to be faking it. They don't just hand out potentially fatal doses of prescription medication like candy, you know." Tomlinson returned the folder to his leather medic's satchel and crossed his legs.

"So, I'm assuming there was nothing untoward in Sylvia's lunch?" Graham asked.

"That fish," Tomlinson confirmed with a flourish, "had not even a passing acquaintance with toxic substances. The food at the White House Inn isn't exactly *cordon bleu*, but it needn't be *cordoned off*, either." Both men allowed themselves a quick chuckle at this dark humor.

"Now, what about her hip pain?" Graham asked.

Tomlinson frowned now. "Severe. Very painful. One look at her hip joints told me there's no way she would voluntarily have navigated a long, stone staircase unless there was George Clooney at the other end."

"Was she on painkillers?"

"Nothing out of the ordinary," Tomlinson answered.

Graham changed tack. "What about the time of death? Were you able to narrow it down?"

"Sorry, old chap. The answer to that little mystery set sail with the tide."

Graham sighed and thought aloud. "A woman is poisoned by something she eats or drinks. Doesn't report it or ask for help. And manages to get down to the beach despite being half crippled, where she's half buried in the sand."

"It's a bugger, isn't it?" Tomlinson offered, standing to leave.

"Yes," Graham answered, distracted. "It most certainly is."

Mrs. Taylor was at pains to point out just how desperately she wanted to help. "But if my paying customers see policemen sniffing around in the kitchen," she said with a worried frown, "they'll head straight for the Bangkok Palace and never eat here again. It's a *full third* of my income each year, that restaurant," she explained.

"Believe me, Mrs. Taylor," Graham told her, "we'll be as discreet as we possibly can. Just being thorough, you know."

They were escorted to the kitchens as though being secreted to the den of a reclusive cult. Mrs. Taylor even stopped at each turn to check the hallway ahead and, at one point, remarked that the "coast was clear." Sergeant Harding found the whole thing highly amusing but hid her giggles behind her uniform sleeve. Her new boss didn't seem to be a man for comedic trifles, nor was she keen to appear girlish and insensitive. Quite the reverse, in fact.

"I'll have the staff come back here to be interviewed," Mrs. Taylor announced as they reached the cool, dry storeroom behind the kitchens. "There are serving hatches that give out onto the dining room from the kitchen, but in here you won't be seen."

Graham recognized from the outset that he would have to indulge Mrs. Taylor's rather paranoid fixation on the delicate sensibilities of her guests. He would admit that seeing uniformed officers snooping around a kitchen was hardly a resounding advertisement for the Inn's culinary fare, but they were just doing their jobs.

Marcella was there, in her late-afternoon role as a waitress and general kitchen helper, as well as five other staff members. Three were long-term employees, and the others had found summer work at the Inn. One had worked there for six holiday seasons in a row. "I like the island, and I like Mrs. Taylor," the young sous-chef told them. "How can you beat sunshine, low taxes, and great beaches just down the steps?"

"How, indeed," Graham commented. "Do you keep records of the guests' breakfast orders, by any chance?"

"Oh, yeah," the chef replied. "We have to, in case there's a billing screw-up." He was quickly able to find Sylvia's order and read it out, as if ordering his staff to prepare it once more. "Muesli, the small fruit platter, toast and marmalade, a boiled egg, tea, and orange juice." He looked up once more. "We squeeze it ourselves, each morning. Absolutely magic."

Graham wrote everything down as usual, the others waiting patiently while he inscribed the details. "And her lunch? Did you prepare that yourself?"

He checked his order slips again, leafing through them. "She's in room two-eleven, right?" He searched on. "Yeah, here she is. Erm... I was doing the vegetable quiche, actually. Her order would have been given to Santi, the other lunch chef. Good guy. His braised beef is the bomb." Then the young chef noticed something else. "Hmm. This might be important."

Harding tilted her head to read the handwriting on the slip. "A glass of Chardonnay?" she asked. She turned the slip to show Graham, whose mind was quickly racing, aware that alcohol was as common a vector for poison as any other.

He looked the chef squarely in the eye. "Who exactly was responsible for the bar at lunchtime?"

Marcella was trembling within a minute of sitting down in the storeroom. "Please understand," Harding was telling her, "you've done nothing wrong. We just need to know about the wine you served to Sylvia. Tell us everything you can remember."

The slender Portuguese girl traced the events in her mind. "I received the order by phone and wrote everything down. I'm sorry for my handwriting," she said with a shy smile. "Then I told the bar I wanted a glass of Chardonnay."

"Did they pour it straight away?" Graham asked, his pen hovering over the surface of the notepad in anticipation.

"I can't remember..." she said at first. "There's always so much things happen. Is so busy and crazy during lunch."

"Take your time, and think back carefully," Sergeant Harding advised her.

Marcella's eyes went misty as she tried to replay every detail. "It was just waiting on the bar top, as normal," she said after a moment. "I put it on the tray with the food, and I think... yes, I walked upstairs because the elevator was so busy."

Graham walked her through those few moments like a hypnotist. "You walked to Sylvia's door... Did you knock as normal?"

"Yes, of course," she said, hearing the sound in her own

mind. "She was maybe on the phone with someone. She said to leave the tray outside."

Sergeant Harding felt, for the first time, the human nature of this loss. A vivacious woman, well liked and romantically involved, simply taken from the world in a blink. "And then?" she asked Marcella.

"I just left the tray and went on to the next delivery. Only a little later, maybe... an hour or two?" she asked, "there was the announcement to the kitchen staff from Mrs. Taylor. She say we should not deliver anything else to two-eleven and should stay away. I was worried," she recalled. "Mrs. Taylor never say anything like this before."

"And that's when you knew something must be wrong?" Graham asked her.

"Poor woman," Marcella sniffed. "I so sorry for her."

Sergeant Harding was as keen as her boss to keep the interview on track. "What about the wine glass, Marcella? What happened to that?"

The girl blinked a few times. "The glass?"

"Yes. It wasn't in the room," Graham told her. "No sign of it."

"But... I deliver the glass of wine with the lunch tray," Marcella insisted. "Was not there?"

Both officers knew that no glass had been found, but Graham felt the need to be absolutely sure. He couldn't risk such a vital piece of evidence being overlooked. "Sergeant, would you ask the forensics team to make a special effort to look for that glass?"

Harding left quietly, and Graham finished up the interview on his own, hoping that being one-on-one with Marcella would neither scare her nor cause her to hide anything. "I need to know just one more thing. Who else had wine with lunch today?"

Marcella brightened. "Oh, is easy. I check the bar receipts. They need to bill the guest, so they always right." She returned thirty seconds later with a stack of slips similar to the restaurant orders the chef had so usefully kept. "Only one!" she reported, handing the slip to Graham.

"Thank you, Marcella. This really is very helpful." Graham took down a note: *Glass of wine, lunchtime. Room two-nineteen. Alice Swift.*"

"No sign of it, sir," Harding reported to her boss in the Inn's lobby. "The team leader says they've turned the place upside down. No wine glass."

"*Bugger*," Graham breathed. "We need to find the other one. This is a real long shot now," he said, glancing at his watch, "but we've got to try." They headed to the kitchens and found the staff busily preparing for dinner. "Marcella?"

Her face fell and brightened only slightly when she saw Sergeant Harding's warm smile. "Is more problems? I told you everything about everything..."

"Please," Graham said. "You're not in any trouble."

Harding said, "It's about the wine glass, Marcella. The one you brought to Alice Swift's room. Do you remember what happened to it?"

She shrugged apologetically and motioned to the big double sink in the corner of the kitchen. "Is cleaned. Everything is cleaned every day before dinner. No mess for the guests to see," she said, her hands sweeping away an imaginary table of dirty dishes. "Chef insists about it."

Harding sent Marcella back to work while Graham took a moment to stand in the corner of the kitchen and swear colorfully under his breath.

"No break there, boss. Sorry," she said, half a second from putting a reassuring hand on his shoulder but wisely thinking better of it.

"No poison in the food," he said, partly to her and partly to himself. "No glass from either room to confirm that was the source. And no witnesses."

Sergeant Harding tried to lift his mood. "You know what Sherlock Holmes would call this kind of case?"

Graham cracked half of a smile, despite himself. "A 'three pipe problem'?" he tried.

"Maybe four. But we'll get to the bottom of it, sir. Don't you worry about that."

Graham took out his notebook and flicked through it, as though the meticulous recording of events might somehow transform themselves into new data. A new theory. A lead, of some sort - of *any* sort.

"I need a cup of tea, Sergeant Harding. Will you join me?"

Despite her initial hopes of seizing her chance to get to know Graham a little better, Harding soon found that this was to be a very quiet, thoughtful cup of tea indeed. Graham barely spoke, and then almost entirely to himself. She was there as a sounding board, her hopes of learning more about this surprisingly sophisticated man dashed almost as soon as they sat down.

"Dead. On the beach. Couldn't have walked there." He took a sip of the tea, and an eyebrow raised in... what was it, recognition? Surprise? It was hard for the Sergeant to say, not knowing him very well. DI Graham put the cup down very carefully, almost soundlessly, and continued. "Hip replacement. Couldn't have managed the steps... Hmm."

The notepad was out again. Harding watched him read

and flick through his notes as she sipped her own tea. It seemed best to say nothing and simply let him think.

"Sort of engaged to the Colonel. Strong chap. Military through and through. But genuinely upset. Wouldn't you say, Janice?"

Sergeant Harding was surprised both to be included in this monologue and to hear Graham call her by her first name. He seemed in another world, caught up in details of murder and suspicion, leads and evidence, people and their potential motives. "I think we can stick with our original thought," she replied, "and rule out the Colonel. A man like him doesn't show his emotions, but we saw enough to know his grief was absolutely real."

"Not a lot of murderers," Graham continued in the same faraway tone, "report the body to the police. Not many at all. They tend to let someone else do that. No, he's in the clear."

More notes, more tea, and more thoughts. "Pilkingtons. She was upset. Furious with him."

"I'm a Dutchman if I understood her reaction," Harding offered.

"Hmm. Dutchman." He was away in a cloudy world of investigative thought.

"Sir?" Sergeant Harding asked, willing this strange monologue to at least begin to make sense.

"They had nothing against her, Harding. She cured the man's cancer, for heaven's sake. A bit of suspicion is one thing, but... do you remember the look on Mrs. Pilkington's face?"

"Again," Harding told him, "that was a genuine reaction. I'm no mind reader, but..."

"No, you're right. They were both telling the truth." His

thoughts meandered silently for a long moment. "Alice. Barely knew her, right?"

"Who, Sylvia?" Harding asked, trying to keep up.

"Headed to London. Sits in her room all day. But had some wine."

"Drinking with lunch, eh?" Harding joked. "Typical creative type."

Graham ignored her, but not unkindly. He was fully occupied, bringing in every detail for this grand synthesis of all they had learned so far. "Where in the seven hells," he said more strongly, "is the wine glass from Sylvia's room?"

Harding thought this over. "Maybe Sylvia's glass was taken away and washed with the rest?" she tried.

Graham finally looked straight at her. "But the tray was still in her room. We *saw* the tray, Sergeant. There was no glass. None."

Feeling foolish, Harding nodded. "I remember now."

"Bugger," Graham said again. "Too many unknowns here. Too many. Except one."

"What's that, Detective Inspector?" she asked, hoping the additional formality might bring him out of his reverie.

"We're officially in a murder inquiry. And," he added with a quirky smile, "I'm not even jolly well unpacked yet. Who ever said that Jersey was some quiet little island?"

Harding drove him back to the station, glancing over at her new boss with growing respect and something more, an admiration which came from watching a fine mind at work. By the time they arrived, she was fizzing with excitement.

CHAPTER FOUR

THE TWO CONSTABLES faced each other across the reception desk, each gesticulating, checking off points on their fingers, holding up a palm to ask for silence, but their clamorous discussion only became audible when Graham and Harding opened the main door to the station.

"All I'm saying is..." Barnwell began.

"If you'll let me finish..." Roach interrupted.

"You're not giving me a chance to make my..."

"Gentlemen," Graham said in a stentorian tone. "Have I wandered, by chance, into the back room of a local pub, or am I, as it truly seems, actually in a... what's it called again, Sergeant... A *police station*?"

"Sorry, sir," the two men said together, eyes downcast like truant schoolboys.

"But don't let me stop you. I just trust that, should a member of the public need either of you, this discussion would be put on hold." Barnwell gave the reception desk's phone a guilty glance. "May I ask what's got you both quite so riled up?"

There was a moment of silence while the two men figured out who was going to speak. "It's this case, sir, at the White House Inn," Barnwell admitted. "We've been mulling it over a bit, that's all."

"Mulling?" Graham replied. "Mulling, you say? Well, I love a good mull." He pulled up a chair in the reception area and sat as though about to watch an engaging documentary. "Mull away, Constables."

Barnwell began. "So, here's what I've been thinking, sir. We know she took some kind of poison, right?" Graham let the Constable continue, despite his stretching the truth from the outset. "She decides to herself, in the middle of doing it, 'Well, I'm about to shuffle off this mortal coil, I may as well have a nice view of the ocean while I'm getting ready to meet my maker'. See?"

"So, it's suicide, you're saying," Graham clarified.

"Yes, sir. She wanders down in a haze of depression and sadness and what-not, and then dies on the beach." He dusted off his hands as though having solved the case at a stroke.

"Constable Roach?" Graham asked. "Do you concur with your colleague?"

Roach cleared his throat. "Begging your pardon sir, but that's bollocks."

Barnwell spun round to confront the younger officer, but Graham cut him off. "Hang on, Barnwell. Let's hear it," he said, motioning to Roach. "But be a good chap and mind your language in front of the Sergeant."

"Sorry, Sarge," Roach said genuinely. "Here's what I'd like to know. How's a lady who's virtually crippled supposed to walk down those steps? Eh? Imagine your Nana trying to do that. She'd bloody well croak on the way down, before she even got to the beach. I don't care what kind of painkillers or whatever it was she was on."

"Interesting point, Constable," Graham said.

"And she's found buried in a sand dune," Roach added. "Who in their right mind walks along a beach, finds a dead lady, and decides, 'Hey, I know, I'll bury this poor woman in the sand, so that the crime scene is well and truly contaminated and the police won't have the first clue as to what happened.' Doesn't make any sense, Barnwell. Think about it."

"The tide!" Barnwell maintained. "Tide comes in, washes the sand over her."

Graham stood and straightened his tie. "I think I'm going to agree with Constable Roach's original assessment of your theory, Barnwell."

"Huh?" Barnwell said.

"The part about it being bollocks," Roach told him in a loud whisper behind his hand.

"It's incomplete," Graham said charitably. "But that doesn't mean you should stop thinking about it. Include this in your mulling, though: *time*. These events actually took place and belong to a point in the pasts of everyone involved. Begin at the time of death and replay the movie backward; who was where, doing what, and why?"

Slightly stunned but thoughtful, the two constables watched Graham and Harding leave. Their Sergeant sported an amused smirk as she accompanied the DI to his office and closed the door.

"I wasn't joking around with them," Graham told her as they sat down in the office. "Well, not entirely."

Harding looked at her watch. She was starting to think about getting home. "They both need a firm hand, from time to time."

"They're fine officers, I'm sure," Graham said. "But investigative policing is an art. Speculating doesn't get you anywhere. It's all about the evidence." He stopped short. "I'm sorry, you know that full well. And you want to get home, obviously, rather than hear me blathering on."

Harding willed herself into silence, though there was much she could say. About how glad she was that this cultured, interesting, competent, charming man had arrived in their midst. About how she felt he would shake up local policing and bring some real professionalism to their rather provincial world.

"I'll be heading home, then. It's been quite a day, hasn't it, sir?" She gave him a friendly smile.

"As first days go, Sergeant, it's been one for the books."

The next morning, Barnwell had only just set up the reception desk for the day when the phone rang.

"Gorey Police Station, Constable Barnwell speaking."

"Ah, good morning. It's DI Graham."

"Morning, boss," Barnwell said brightly. "You're up early."

Graham ignored the remark. This was, Barnwell found, a trait of the DI's. He was all business, no chit-chat. No time to shoot the breeze when there was a murderer on the loose. "Let's meet in the lobby of the White House Inn as soon as you can get here, Barnwell. Leave the desk to Roach. I've got an assignment for you."

As he replaced the receiver, Barnwell couldn't help but think, with an enjoyable jolt of *Schadenfreude*, just how jealous Roach would be. Perhaps Graham's arrival was *his* passport to promotion and security. A couple of decent performances on the job, and he might even be made Sergeant once Janice moved on. It was a heady thought.

Barnwell found Graham hard at work in the lobby, despite the early hour. "It's true what they say about birds and worms, Constable Barnwell," Graham assured his colleague. "People's memories tend to be at their freshest after a good night's sleep. That initial boost of sugar and a strong cup of tea can do wonders for recall," he said, toasting Barnwell with a fine china cup. It brimmed with a hard-to-find Japanese tea, redolent with the scents of a misty meadow. "It's amazing what details we'll hear today that were unavailable just a few hours ago."

Mrs. Taylor emerged from the office, looking fresh from the shower. "No cancellations last night, I'm happy to say!" she reported, bustling around her office and then heading into the dining room to check on preparations for breakfast. Barnwell followed Graham, who was peppering the proprietor with questions, toward the smells of bacon, eggs, and sausage. His stomach growled plaintively. He'd planned to grab his usual, leisurely mid-morning bacon sandwich at the St. George Café near the station, but with Graham's diligent attitude to the morning hours, there simply wouldn't be time.

His daydream of a plate piled high with cooked breakfast was disturbed by the demands of his profession. "Barnwell, I want you to investigate the Pilkingtons, Alice Swift, and the Colonel until you're certain that you know every detail of what they did yesterday between the hours of ten and two." Barnwell's shoulders swept back, and his spine straightened like that of a parading soldier. "Leave nothing to chance. No detail is too small, no finding irrelevant until proved so. I need to know how well they all knew each other, and especially, for how *long*. You with me?"

"Yes, sir," Barnwell snapped out. "I'll get right on that."

"Well," Graham said, checking his watch. "Maybe let them get out of bed first. It's not even seven."

"Will do, sir," Barnwell said, slightly less martially. "What about Constable Roach?"

"I've got something else in mind for him. Just stick to those four people like glue, and write down *everything*," Graham told him. Then there was a cheeky grin. "You can, can't you?"

"Sir?"

"*Write*, Barnwell."

"Yes, sir," the Constable replied, entirely without irony.

"I'm pulling your leg, man." Barely even a smile. Graham shrugged off the urge to sigh at the man's plodding, unimaginative sincerity. *It takes all sorts to make a police force. And this kind of assignment should sort the police from the sort-of police*, he mused silently. "Off you go, then. Remember, every detail written down. See you about lunchtime." He gave Barnwell a comradely chuck on the shoulder. "Come and get me if you discover something momentous."

Graham spent a few more minutes striding through the hotel alongside the perpetual whirlwind of morning energy that was Mrs. Taylor. She wasn't meaning to be unhelpful, the proprietor explained, she was just trying to run a busy hotel in the summer. Graham ascertained that she'd told him every last useful thing, expressed his gratitude once more, and retreated to the lobby.

Sergeant Harding was already in the back office, checking their list of interviewees. "You know, there's one guest we haven't spoken to at all yet. This guy," she said, tapping the list. "Likes to set up his meal reservations in advance," she said, proud of this modest piece of sleuthing.

Graham thought for a moment. "Set up an interview, Sergeant. Let's see what he has to say for himself."

A few hours later, Carlos Alves was sitting in a deck chair on the Inn's garden terrace, overlooking a calm sea which sparkled in mid-morning sunshine. Cigar smoke wafted on the breeze. He had thick, black hair that made its own decisions. He wore a white, cotton summer shirt and Chinos. As he rose to shake Graham's hand, the Inspector judged him to be a little over fifty, but in good shape, and with surprisingly rough hands.

"I take it that you sail," Graham said after the pleasantries were exchanged.

Carlos glanced down at his hands and smiled. "Perhaps it doesn't take a detective to know this, eh? I have a motor-sailer, thirty-four foot, harbored in Cowes. I like to sail between the islands in the summer. Normally, I stay on Guernsey or Sark. I like the quiet there."

For a mainlander like Graham, even one who grew up in the remoteness of the Yorkshire dales, the idea of spending extended time somewhere *smaller* than Jersey was close to unimaginable. Sark was barely bigger than his own village back home. "Beautiful islands," he said neutrally.

"Maybe you are surprised," he guessed. "Why don't I go down to the Greek Islands or the Pacific, no?"

Graham shrugged slightly. "We all tend to end up wherever makes us the most happy."

A change came over Carlos' face, and it became stern and businesslike. "You are here," he said in his most serious tone yet, "about the death of Dr. Norquist, yes?"

"That's correct," Graham said. "We're interviewing everyone at the hotel, and..."

"I'm glad she's dead," Carlos said. He looked away at the ocean, then back at Graham, as if challenging him to make an accusation.

"I'm sorry, Mr. Alves?" Graham asked, shocked. The case seemed to crack wide open.

"She was a terrible woman." He raised a finger as if in warning. "And a *dangerously* incompetent doctor."

Graham wrote down every word, wishing for once that he had some recording technology to capture this moment of confession. "I'm listening," was all he said.

Carlos sighed deeply. "But I did not kill her."

Graham's whole physicality seemed to sag under him. *Bugger*. "But you knew her well?"

"Well enough," he explained, taking a long sequence of puffs on his cigar, as though the nicotine hit might steel him for this emotionally fraught discussion. "She was the doctor of my son. His name was Juan-Carlos."

Again, no detective's badge was needed to discern quite what had happened. "I'm sorry, Mr. Alves." He felt it better to ask less and simply listen.

"He was sixteen years old. Can you imagine that, Inspector?" Carlos asked, his face etched with pain now. "He was healthy, happy. Full of life. He played soccer for his school. Was chasing girls all the time," he said with a nostalgic smile. "Then he says he finds problems in walking. His legs won't do as they're told," he explained. "Then his vision becomes strange, seeing two of everything. Then at dinner times," Carlos went on, "he can't swallow, almost choking on his food."

"It sounds terrible," Graham said consolingly.

"Our doctor, he didn't really know. But there were tests,

and tests and *more* tests," Carlos said, reducing a year of worry and heartache and despair to a few words, "and they find a tumor. Here," he said, fingers at the very back of his neck, where the spine meets the skull.

"A brain stem tumor?" Graham asked gently.

"Is treatable, but is difficult," Carlos continued. "You need *real professional*," he said, fist in his palm, every syllable clear. "The *best*."

"And so you first met Sylvia."

Carlos nodded, and then lifted the cigar to his mouth again but stopped short, gave Graham a rueful, slightly ashamed look, and placed it back in its ashtray, forgotten. "My wife, Gloria. She has a friend whose baby girl had the cancer... Oh, Inspector, the most terrible kind. Of the *eye*," he said, pained at the memory. "Two years old. But Sylvia was assigned to the little girl, and she *survived*!"

"Medical science is remarkable," Graham commented.

"Ah, no," Carlos said, hands aloft. "This was not just science, according to my Gloria. No, no," he said, shaking his head in wonder. "This was *Jesus*. She was as certain of this as we are certain that we're on Jersey. She was *absolutely convinced* that the sacred spirit came down and saved that little girl. The spirit, working through Sylvia. Do you understand?"

With his parents' relaxed attitude to church-going, particularly as their children grew older and found other ways to spend their Sunday mornings, Graham had never been a devoted man of faith, but he respected the sincerity of those who were. "I think so, sir."

"Gloria insisted on having Sylvia as our doctor. And if you ever met her, you would know that if she *insists* on something, it's *gonna happen*, you know?" he chuckled. "No matter that Sylvia wasn't a specialist in brain cancers. No, it would be Jesus guiding her hands, and he would deliver our son from this devil-cancer. You see?"

Graham could see mostly how a family was torn apart by grief and by the tragic results of a poor decision. He could also see that his initial hopes of hearing a confession were being well and truly dashed. If anyone he'd so far met possessed a comprehensible reason to want Sylvia dead, it was this man. However, to Graham, this did not sound even a little like the confession of a murderer.

"Sylvia studied and practiced and got advice from everyone," Carlos explained. "She made it her life for *months*, to attack this difficult and complex cancer like a battle, like she was fighting for her own life, you know?"

"But, despite her efforts, the treatment failed?" Graham asked with all the sensitivity he could find.

"She should have refused to treat him. She didn't know what she was doing."

Carlos stood and made for the ocean, but after a few steps, stopped and turned. "You know, I understand boats. And shipping, you know, freight and that kind of business. But I became an *expert* on the human brain stem. I could give you a lecture right now," he assured the detective, "like a professional, on every aspect of it. But to put it in a few words: the treatment didn't work, and my son died."

"A most dreadful tragedy."

"And it *could* have happened to any patient, treated by any doctor. But it happened to *my* son, treated by *her*." The pain, Graham could plainly see, was undimmed by the passing of time, and seemingly not even a little assuaged by the death of Dr. Norquist.

"Mr. Alves," Graham began, "I'm sure you realize how this might seem, to an investigator."

"I'm a grieving father, Inspector," Carlos said. "Not a

fool."

"Then... I must ask if you know anything that might help with our inquiries?"

Carlos reclaimed the cigar, shaking his head. "I was on Guernsey yesterday, Detective. I sailed back overnight. It's my favorite time to sail, in the cool and the dark. Nobody else around." He puffed on the cigar. "There are harbormaster's records on both sides," he assured Graham.

"I have no reason to suspect you're being dishonest with me, sir. But I have to admit you do have a pretty strong motive."

"And perhaps," Carlos said, cigar aloft in an expansive gesture, "a jury would not send me to jail. But imagine if they *did*. I'm fifty-three years old. I would be an old man when I got out, if I ever did. I could not sacrifice my remaining years, all of the time I have left with my Gloria, who is already without her son, just to punish this woman. I could *not*."

Another page was filled with cursive handwriting. Carlos used the silence to say something that stilled Graham's hand.

"I shouldn't say this," Carlos said, tapping off the cigar ash, "but I wish to express my thanks to whoever is responsible for this crime. Truly. I ask God's forgiveness for this, but it is how I feel." He stopped, puffed once more. "Are you a father, Detective?"

For barely a second, Graham paused in his writing, his eyes clouding over. He shook his head, "No".

"Hold them close," Carlos said, his eyes glistening. "You never know how long they will have." With that, he turned back toward the ocean, his cigar lodged between his lips now, puffing intently, watching the sailboats rounding the headland at the tip of the beach.

"Thank you for your time." Graham stood and headed straight back inside, filling in his notebook quickly, before the memories faded.

Graham drank tea with a mechanical, heedless air, sitting alone in the Inn's tea room. It was fairly quiet, perhaps half an hour before the lunch crowd would begin to arrive. And rather than bringing together the facts in an orderly, determined way as he had before, Graham was letting the thoughts come as they may. The tea helped, as it always did. Perhaps the sea air, also. Sometimes, he found, an investigator needed to simply shut up and allow a well-trained mind to do its work.

"Constable Roach?"

The young officer was standing discreetly in the lobby, almost hidden by a giant coat stand. "Morning, sir."

"I need you to do something for me." Moments later, Roach was on his way down to the harbormaster's office, searching for news of an arrival early this morning. Graham believed that he knew genuine grief and a genuine story when he experienced them, but he'd never be able to look his colleagues in the eye if Carlos turned out to be the murderer and all Graham had done was sit with the man for a sympathetic chat.

"Sergeant Harding, do you have a phone that can play videos?"

Harding proudly showed him her phone, one of the latest models. It had cost well over a week's salary and worked like a charm. Graham explained what he wanted, and they sat together to review some of the search results.

"You see, we've been going about this all wrong,"

Graham told her. "We'd assumed that the journey from here at the Inn," he said, tracing the path on the table in front of him with his finger, "down to the beach would have been awkward and painful for Sylvia."

"I'm sure it would," Harding agreed.

"But what if..." he said, turning the phone to give them a larger view. "What if it were absolutely *impossible*?"

The video showed part of the trials of a new drug. A lady of Sylvia's age, perhaps a year or two older, was struggling to walk. Sweating, pale, and in immense pain, she could barely take three steps together, on level ground, clasping a handrail as though she would drown without it. "Sergeant," he said with a smirk, "I don't know how often you find yourself saying this, but..."

"Constable Roach was right," she conceded. "There's no way on God's green earth that Sylvia Norquist walked down those steps. No way at all." Harding raced to put two and two together. "So she was *carried*?"

"In broad daylight. At lunchtime. On a beach at the tail end of summer." Graham grimaced. "That, believe it or not, is our best theory, as it stands."

Harding thought for a second, then shut down the phone and looked square at her boss. "If I may quote the distinguished philosopher, Jim Roach, sir... I think that's bollocks."

Constable Barnwell checked in throughout the day. He was a little like a child sent off to find the toothpaste aisle in the supermarket but uncertain whether his parents would still be there when he got back. Although unused to individual responsibility, the Constable was proving himself a surprisingly tenacious investigator, and Graham was pleased to see him writing reams of notes.

His more responsible colleague, Constable Roach, had also done his best for the new boss. Carlos Alves had, in fact, traveled back from Guernsey that very morning, and the particulars of his stay on Jersey's sister island and his smart sailboat all checked out. Graham could not rule Alves out of the investigation entirely, as he would have preferred, however. The history between Alves and the deceased was far too compelling for that, but Graham could at the very least put aside suspicion of any direct involvement in the killing. Besides, Graham pondered over yet another pot of fine tea later that afternoon, Alves was neither the kind of man, nor was he carrying the kind of grudge that spoke to poisoning as the preferred method of murder. He could well imagine a calculating, incensed Alves beating Sylvia to death or strangling her as he watched the last light leave her eyes, but not poisoning.

No. Something else was going on, and they were still some way from what any investigator worth their salt would call a "lead." Graham finished the tea, feeling energized, quick of mind, and light of feet as he often did at these times, and called Dr. Tomlinson.

"Do call me Marcus, old chap. I have a feeling we'll be spending a great deal of time together, and I don't hold with needless formality," Dr. Tomlinson told him.

"Marcus it is, although I'm sorry to disturb you so late in the day. Do you have plans for dinner?" Graham wondered.

"Thought you'd never ask."

Two hours later, in a quiet corner of the Bangkok Palace, the two men were being served cold, crisp Thai lager and an initial snack of sticky rice that came with an incautiously ferocious dip called *jaew bong*. Fearless of spicy food, Graham found to his delight that the innocuous-looking dip was laced with pungent shallots and searing chilies.

Tomlinson, far more wary, resolved to dip each ball of rice only fleetingly into its midst. "Christ alive," he muttered. "I might be too old for this kind of thing. How about a nice, uneventful coconut curry?" he asked the waiter. Graham ordered something that was marked with three chilies on the menu, and the waiter gave him a knowing smile, as if both impressed at Graham's audacity and slightly fearful for his continued wellbeing.

"So, I suppose we're all rather curious," Tomlinson began. "What brings an accomplished Detective Inspector like yourself..."

"To a quiet, provincial backwater like this?" Graham smiled.

"Well, something like that. It's hardly a hotbed of ambition. Gorey Constabulary, I mean. The previous DI was in his position for sixteen years, between here and Guernsey, and showed absolutely no interest in ascending the ladder of investigative greatness," Tomlinson explained. "He fit right in."

"But surely," Graham countered, "Jersey is full of aspirational young people? Didn't I read that the economy is booming?"

"The *banking* sector, yes! The *police* sector, not so much." The waiter set the steaming, aromatic coconut curry before the doctor, who inhaled the vapors with relish. "With so little to challenge them, beyond the odd missing person, the local force has been resting on its laurels pretty much continuously since the Newall murders. Even the cases involving corrupt bankers, that kind of thing, get sent over the water to the financial crime boffins who work on the mainland."

"Resting on their laurels, you say. I guess that includes Roach and Barnwell?" Graham asked as his own seafood curry arrived. Its deep, glossy redness gave ample warning of the raging fires within.

"They're good lads," Tomlinson chuckled. "I was a little nervous of having them work on a murder investigation like this, but I'm sure they'll do you proud. Just don't count on miraculous flashes of insight from either of them."

"I won't," he said, trying the curry. It was excellent and supremely hot.

"So beyond joining a booming economy, what brought you down here?" Tomlinson asked again. It was a persistence born not of an impolite, gossipy impulse, but of a genuine curiosity. Graham was so unlike his predecessor, far better trained, and much more polished and assured, that his presence seemed, at first glance, almost strange. In fact, Tomlinson had already dismissed the notion that Graham was sent down *specifically because* Sylvia Norquist's murder was anticipated by someone in the London hierarchy. And *that* had sent him on a five-minute reverie that would have produced a pretty good plot for one of the thriller novels Tomlinson was known to pen in his free time.

"The job came up," Graham said simply, "and I applied."

"But why?" Tomlinson pressed.

"Change of scenery, I suppose. A new challenge."

Tomlinson set down his spoon and dabbed his mouth with his napkin. "Challenge?"

"Sure."

"Dear chap, your main challenge, this highly unusual

murder aside, will be to keep yourself busy! You know that Roach plays solitaire on the reception desk for about three hours of each shift? And that Barnwell..." He paused. "I shouldn't tell tales out of school."

"He drinks," Graham said. "There's a look in the eye. I recognize it all too well." Something in Graham's tone, a firm undercurrent of seriousness, told Tomlinson both that he knew what he was talking about, and that the experiences may well have been first-hand. On this matter, wisely, the doctor did not press further.

A change of subject was in order. "Is there a Mrs. Graham?" he asked with a raised eyebrow.

"There was," Graham told him, and Tomlinson immediately regretted the question. It did not take much digging, it seemed, to reveal the complexities of this new man. It wasn't that Tomlinson didn't accept Graham's reasoning for transferring to this rural idyll. It just made more sense if there were deeper reasons. Perhaps, he wondered, Graham had been pushed as much as pulled toward an obscure assignment like this one. But if so, why not Scotland or a quiet Sussex village?

"I'm sorry," Tomlinson said openly. "None of my business."

"We were heading in different directions," Graham said next. "We had very different priorities."

"Well, whatever your priorities *aren't*, I'd say that you've already shown yourself to be an assiduous and competent detective," Tomlinson said, raising a glass in salute to the new DI.

"Too kind, Marcus." Graham paused. "I guess that means you can call me David.

"I will, if I may. The previous DI went by 'Buster,' but I hardly think that fits you."

Graham took a moment to laugh it out. The more he learned about his predecessor, the more he seemed the typically comical, buffoonish, rural cop stereotype. Seriously overweight, according to Harding. Lax with his personal hygiene, according to Barnwell, who himself didn't smell as though he'd just stepped off the set of a deodorant commercial. "Sounds like quite the character," was Graham's compromised response.

"A big pair of shoes to fill." Both men laughed now, the ice thoroughly broken. Tomlinson was glad to see the younger man enjoying himself and the indelicate questions about his past forgotten.

But it didn't take Graham long to get back to business. "I'm afraid we have to talk about this blessed case," Graham said, pouring Tomlinson some more beer.

"Fire away, Detective Inspector. I'm as puzzled as you are, if I'm plain."

"What's really bothering me at the moment," Graham explained, "except for who might have killed her, of course, is the *timing*."

Tomlinson stirred the remaining third of his curry with his spoon. "Hmm?" he asked.

"She was found dead a couple of hours after lunch, right?" His colleague nodded, his mouth full of lightly-spiced chicken. "So we assumed that the poison was delivered with lunch. Poor Marcella seems to have been the unwitting accessory."

"That's as far as I'd got, too," Tomlinson confirmed.

"But you pinned her death to within an eighteen hour period. So, what if," Graham asked, pointing his chopsticks at Tomlinson, "she was murdered the previous night and carried down the stairs?"

Tomlinson washed down the curry with a long pull on

his beer before answering. "Buried in the dark, when nobody was about?" he conjectured. "Makes more sense than the murderer lugging a dead or dying Sylvia down those steps in broad daylight."

"And what about the poison?" Graham pressed.

"Yes, I was coming to that. I reviewed some old textbooks, and you know, there actually aren't a lot of poisons that leave so few signs for the post-mortem. The classics," he said, ticking them off on his fingers, "are strychnine, cyanide, and arsenic. They all leave tell-tale indications of their role."

Graham made a wheeling motion with his chopsticks as he braved the nuclear firestorm that was his red seafood curry.

"Strychnine, for example, causes convulsions that leave the body locked in an arched position. Cyanide leaves a smell of bitter almonds, famously," he added. "But our Sylvia seems to have died from something that pretty quickly stopped her heart and her breathing without leaving much evidence behind."

"So, what are you thinking?" Graham asked, pausing to draw cool air across a scorched tongue.

"Haven't a clue, old chap. Give me another day to check with some colleagues in the business and to continue the postmortem."

The returning waiter heard the term and blanched slightly. "Is everything to your satisfaction, gentlemen?" he asked warily.

"Only one thing," Graham asked, now visibly sweating. "Next time I come in," he said, pausing again to bring cool air into his mouth, "could you make mine a little hotter?"

CHAPTER FIVE

SERGEANT JANICE HARDING hovered uncertainly at the big double doors. Despite the authority of her rank and uniform, it was hard to shake the feeling that she was trespassing. The hallway was brightly lit but exceedingly quiet, not only because of the early hour, but also because not one of the "patients" in this part of the hospital would ever make a single sound again.

"Isn't this a little... unorthodox?" she asked DI Graham as he confidently swept down the hallway. Barnwell and Roach followed behind, Roach looking positively exhilarated.

"We're police officers, Sergeant," he reminded her. "Police work has its dull moments and its exciting parts. And it also inevitably has things like this."

Graham pushed open the doors and found Dr. Tomlinson, clipboard in hand, standing by a mortuary table. He wore a face mask, and motioned for all four of his visitors to don them before continuing. Barnwell needed some assistance with his but got there in the end. Before them was a sight which brought different reactions from each officer.

"I'd like to introduce Dr. Sylvia Norquist," Tomlinson said with a singularly inappropriate flourish and brought back the white sheet to reveal the corpse. Harding's hand flew to her mouth. Barnwell stared as though in the audience at a freak show. And Roach's eyes narrowed studiously. For him, this was a learning opportunity and not one that was likely to come around very often.

"Asphyxia, ladies and gentlemen. A dangerous constriction of the supply of oxygen to the brain, causing unconsciousness and death. This was the chief cause of Sylvia's demise."

"But," Graham said, continuing the explanation, "asphyxia doesn't *explain* her death. It merely gives us the final reason why she expired. Every asphyxia has a cause. Not to sound like we're in medical school right now or anything, but could you name some?" Graham asked the trio of officers.

Roach raised a hand before Graham gave him a look. "Strangulation," he offered.

"That's one," Tomlinson agreed.

"Smothering?" Harding tried.

"That's another," Graham replied.

"Depressurization? Like, on a plane?" Barnwell said next.

"Sure. Other things are likely to kill you just as quickly way up there, but okay," Tomlinson allowed. "But there are no signs of smothering, no paleness in the skin around the nose and mouth. No ligature markings," he said, his pencil at Sylvia's neck to illustrate the point, "which might indicate strangulation. And she certainly wasn't on a plane when she died. So..."

"What else causes asphyxia," Roach thought aloud, "but doesn't leave any traces?"

"Here come two big words that I want you to get used to," Tomlinson warned. "Tachycardic arrhythmia." He paused. "Anyone want to try making sense of that?"

Graham chuckled. "From medical school to linguistics class in one swift leap. Why do we do *cardio* exercise?"

"To get our heart's racing," Harding offered, remembering her fitness instructor's stern insistences.

"Excellent. And what might an 'arrhythmia' be?" Graham asked.

"Like a rhythm?" Roach tried.

"Yes, but in this case," Tomlinson said, his hand aloft in a lightly closed fist, "a *lack* of rhythm." He pumped the fist in a steady pulse, but then it shuddered and failed, restarted and stopped again, jumping like a scratched record. "Something made her heart beat so abnormally unrhythmically that it fatally compromised her ability to breathe."

Barnwell was fixated on the pulsing fist. "So, she went and had a heart attack and asphyxiated, *at the same time*?"

"Well, one came as a result of the other, but you've got the idea, young man," Tomlinson told him. "So... *What* was it? What could possibly make a healthy human heart behave like this?"

All three stared down at the spotless, white tiles in thoughtful puzzlement. "Electricity?" Harding said first.

"There would be characteristic burning under her skin," Tomlinson said.

"No stab wounds or signs that she was hit by anything? Roach said.

"Not even a little bit. No signs of struggle in her room, either," Graham said.

Then Barnwell lit up. "*Poison*. You suspected that all along, didn't cha?"

Graham clapped the Constable on the shoulder and gave Tomlinson a wink. "Marcus, would you be good enough to introduce these fine officers to the murder weapon in this case?"

They could not have been more keyed up if Sherlock Holmes were walking them through his deductions. "*Aconitum variegatum*," Tomlinson announced, bringing from behind the table a small bunch of delicate, purple-blue flowers. "Of the order *Ranunculales*, but of course you knew that," he grinned.

"A *plant* did this to her?" Harding gasped.

"Not just any plant," Tomlinson told them, passing each a stalk topped with a group of the flowers. "You can see how it gets one of its colloquial names, 'Monkshood.'"

Even at first glance, they could. The center of each flower was protected by a tall, drooping, purple hood, and pairs of petals on either side. "They're rather pretty," Harding said. "Almost like something my grandmother would have in her garden."

"Oh, I agree," Tomlinson said. "But like most colorful, attractive things in nature, the color is there as a warning. These things," he said, taking the stalks back as though removing unlit sparklers from lighter-toting teenagers, "are bloody deadly. Mash up a big handful of these stalks and petals, dissolve the results in alcohol, and you have something called 'tincture of aconite', otherwise known as Wolfsbane."

"Sounds like something out of Harry Potter, doesn't it?" Graham quipped. "But it's real, and it's not nice at all."

"Slip even a *teaspoon* of your tincture into someone's drink," Tomlinson told them, "and your victim would be as dead as a doornail inside four or six hours, tops. But it doesn't show up on a toxicology screen and leaves behind neither a smell nor color that a post-mortem might pick up."

"Wow," Roach breathed.

"Indeed, Constable. It's not something," Tomlinson said with a tone of pride, "that your garden-variety pathologist would have spotted. There were few signs, you see. Tiny amounts of foam. Not many things make us *literally* 'foam at the mouth.'"

"I suppose not," Harding said, eyeing the corpse warily.

"And then we found that her stomach was entirely empty. That's normally only as a result of having vomited very heavily. If someone is poisoned," Tomlinson told them, "this can be the best thing for them."

"Aren't you supposed to... whatcha call it," Barnwell was saying, "*induce* vomiting?"

"You are," the pathologist agreed. "And she did. But not fast enough, unfortunately. I could tell from the way the sand clung to her that she'd been sweating before her death. All these symptoms are indicative of poisoning by *aconitum* or Wolfsbane," he concluded, satisfied with his own work.

Graham took over again. "The poison also causes the heart problems we talked about. This, in turn, stopped Sylvia's breathing and caused the asphyxia. Can you believe that growing and owning the plants, even the tincture, is perfectly legal?"

"It's been used for centuries in Chinese traditional medicine," Tomlinson added. "And aromatherapy. Quite safe on the skin, but damned near always fatal if you're dosing someone's drink with it."

Barnwell's fingers clicked. "The Chardonnay."

Roach stared at his colleague as though he'd stolen his girlfriend, but Graham was impressed. "The Chardonnay, and the glass it was in. Those are the most promising pieces of evidence, but there's no bloody sign of them."

Tomlinson covered the body. "Not yet, anyway. Fingers crossed, eh?" He thanked the team and ushered them out. "Keep in touch, David. We're getting close, I can feel it."

The four talked the matter through all the way back to the station and then in an animated, focused huddle in DI Graham's small office. Graham was anxious to know what Barnwell had learned during the previous day's sleuthing. "I saw you striding around that hotel with a purposeful air, Constable. What did you discover?"

Barnwell flipped through his notebook. "It's pretty much as we expected, sir. The Pilkingtons, well... They're a funny pair, sir. Very argumentative at the moment. She's furious with him for hiding the return of his cancer and for spending time with Sylvia without her knowing."

"How did you find out all that?" Roach wanted to know.

"Easy. You just stand behind a potted fern," Barnwell explained, "looking like you're doing nothing except guarding the lobby, and you keep your ears open. People will say all sorts in front of a stationary copper. It's like you're not even there."

"Any indication that Mrs. Pilkington might have hurt Sylvia?" Graham asked, though he was pretty certain of the answer.

"No, sir. The way I see it, she's angry about this for the first time, not the second, if you see what I mean." Graham was nodding. "If she'd killed Sylvia, would she still be giving her husband daily bollockings for having had coffee with her?"

"Good point," Harding observed. "What else?"

"There's that South American bloke, Carlos Alves,"

Barnwell reported. "He was down at the marina for a while, but he spent almost the whole time on the terrace, just staring out to sea."

"He's got a lot on his mind," Graham informed them.

"Such as?" Roach asked, irritated to be playing second fiddle to the likes of Barnwell. "Guilt, maybe?"

"His son died," Graham said.

"On Sylvia's watch," Barnwell reminded them. "I checked and there was a question of negligence, of not being up to the job. It was in the papers at the time. There was an internal investigation, but they decided against suspending her or taking it further. His wife," Barnwell said, then whistled, "sounds like *quite* the character. Wouldn't want to get on the wrong side of her. They're an odd couple, right enough."

"Grief," Graham commented quietly, "does terrible things to relationships."

Only Harding spotted the distant, despondent look on his face, but she said nothing.

"Doesn't that make him our prime suspect, sir?" Barnwell asked. "There's certainly motive, wouldn't you say?"

"I would, but I interviewed him in detail, and I see no reason to suspect that he's here to do anything but sail his boat and stare at the sea. He's grieving, not vengeful. Not actively, anyway."

Roach joined Barnwell's protests. "Seriously, sir, I think we should consider him. I mean, we all read your notes, right?" The others nodded. "Didn't he say that he's glad she died?"

"He said that. But he didn't kill her," Graham replied. "Leave him for now. What about the others?"

"Alice Swift keeps to herself. She was in her room for almost the whole day. Came down for morning tea but had lunch and dinner brought to her room by Marcella," Barnwell said.

"She's working on a tapestry," Graham explained. "A very gifted lady."

Harding frowned but quickly regained her composure. "No indication that she's mourning. It's not clear that she even knew Sylvia," she commented. "We can probably just rule her out."

"Who did she have tea with?" Graham asked.

"Er... Colonel Graves," Barnwell said, consulting his notes.

The conversation stopped. "Wait, they *know* each other?" Harding asked.

Barnwell checked his notes. "They talked about money, that was all I could gather. It was hard to hear," he reported. "There were other people around and they were leaning in close, you know."

"Money?" Roach wondered aloud. "What's the Colonel doing, now he's retired from the army?"

"Real estate investments, across the pond," Graham told him. "Maybe Alice and he are in business together. She seemed wealthy enough, right, Sergeant?"

"Wealthy enough to speculatively open a niche weaving business in a ritzy, expensive part of London," she remarked. "Certainly didn't seem like she was short of a penny."

"What about Sylvia?" Graham said. "She wasn't exactly poor, either."

"I mean," Harding said next, "anyone who's staying at the White House Inn has got a good chunk of cash under their mattress, that's for certain. What does Mrs. Taylor charge her long-termers, maybe £70 a night?"

"About that. Or maybe a little more," Graham confirmed.

"Here's a theory," Barnwell began. "The Colonel is in financial trouble, right? Housing market over in the States takes a dip or whatever. He asks Sylvia for a loan, and she says no."

"Go on," Graham said, a little skeptical already.

"So he's putting pressure on her to show him that she loves him, that she trusts him, you know, by giving him money. But it all falls apart between them because she won't fork over the cash, and he's short on the mortgages or whatever, so his properties are at risk of being foreclosed on."

It was a more thorough theory than Graham had initially expected, but it wasn't without weaknesses. "And so..."

"So, he poisons her. End of story."

Barnwell sat back, a look of pride settling across his face.

"Well, that was anti-climactic," Harding grumbled.

"Got a better suggestion?" Barnwell shot back.

"Take it easy, Constable," Graham told him, but kept his tone light. The man was trying his best, he could see. "We've already satisfied ourselves that Colonel Graves is genuinely grieving."

Barnwell shrugged. "Can't you grieve for someone's death, even though you're responsible for it?"

"That's pushing it a bit," Roach argued. "I mean, the bloke was properly upset. You heard his voice on the phone, right when he found her. You said he was devastated."

"And," Harding said, finger aloft, "we already know how frequently the murderer calls in the body. Right, sir?"

"Right, Sergeant," Graham agreed. "It's not 'never,' but it's pretty rare."

"Bugger," Barnwell cursed. "Thought I was onto something, didn't I?"

Graham gave him a consoling look. "Keep doing what you're doing, Constable. We'll crack it, I promise."

Barnwell wasn't ready to give up just yet. "Couldn't we talk to him, one more time?" he asked. "I mean, it's just the way they were sitting together, leaning close, keeping their voices down, in the tea room. It just... I don't know, it just seemed *odd*."

Roach couldn't resist. "Well, you'd know *odd* when you saw it."

Barnwell ignored him. "Sir? How about it?"

Graham was on his feet. "We'll crack this case by being thorough. Let's do it."

"Righto," Barnwell said, giving Roach a provocative look before following his boss out to the car.

"You drive," Graham ordered. "I'll call him."

Barnwell drove with deliberate care and attention, partly to impress Graham, but also because of the number of tourists, often woefully unfamiliar with Jersey's driving code, milling around and slowing everyone down. *As usual.*

"I wouldn't have thought of that, boss," he said.

"Hmm?" Graham replied. He'd been writing in his notebook once more.

"Inviting the Colonel to dinner. It's a nice touch, given what he's been through this week."

Graham clicked his pen closed and slotted the notebook away. It had become the most fluid of actions, done almost without thought, like changing gear or shaving. "It's not purely charity, Constable. People tend to say more when they believe they are not under suspicion. As far as the Colonel is concerned, we're just ascertaining background details."

The White House Inn was busy, but Mrs. Taylor found Graham and Graves the quietest table still available, on the terrace overlooking the English Channel. Carlos Alves was there once more, smoking a cigar. He nodded gravely but politely to the two men and carried on his evening vigil, scanning the waves as though the happiness so brutally stolen from him might somehow emerge from the deep.

"I'll take a dry sherry," Graves told Marcella. "And for you?" The Colonel looked at DI Graham.

"Oh, just water. Thanks, Marcella." Marcella glided away.

The two men looked at each other. "I actually wanted to begin by thanking you," Graham said. "Your assistance has been invaluable in this investigation."

Graves was surprised. "I only did what anyone would do. There might be," he speculated, "some kind of closure for me in finding whoever did this."

"Well, we're getting closer all the time," Graham assured him. "Look, I'm sorry if this is indelicate, but..."

"Please," Graves said, his palms open.

"It's about your real estate investments. You mentioned them briefly when we last spoke. Can you say a little more about your portfolio?"

Graves took a sip of his sherry and then smiled. "Looking to invest, Detective?"

"On *my* salary?" Graham snorted. "Hardly."

"Well, here's how I've been working it," he said, setting down his glass on the pure white tablecloth. "I put up a good portion of the money to buy a nice, high-end, beachfront property near Miami, for example. Perfect for a young lawyer who wants a view of the ocean, that kind of client."

"I see," Graham said. "You don't mind if I take notes? Just routine," he assured the Colonel.

"Not a bit. But no stealing my investment ideas! I worked bloody hard for that money." Starters arrived, and Marcella was gone in a second.

"So you're one of several investors?"

"That's right," Graves said, stabbing a shred of romaine lettuce with his fork. "We all pitch in together, do the place up, get a local agent to generate some interest among the right crowd, and then they sell it for us. They get a cut, and after all the taxes and what-not, we divide the rest."

"And how many of you are there?" Graham asked. His carrot and ginger soup was rather tasty, he found.

"Seven, this time around. So we're looking to clear probably..." He calculated in his head. "About thirty thousand dollars profit, each. Maybe a little more. Then we go again. I only deal in cash, you see. I'd never borrow to front a property deal."

"Why not?" Graham asked. "Most people do."

Graves chuckled. "Not me, old chap. Too wise," he said, tapping his nose. "If everything goes belly up, I'd owe some blood-sucking bank a sodding fortune with nothing to sell except the shirt off my back. Put my all into this, I did."

"Why take the risk?" Graham asked.

"All I really wanted," Graves said, his face falling, "was to do a few good deals over there, cash in, and marry Sylvia. We'd get ourselves a nice little cottage somewhere like this," he said, glancing out into the bay, "and just live out our lives together." The sadness permeated him now, and Graham felt for the man. A life of service and sacrifice, and now there would be no one to share the remainder with, and only precarious overseas investments to keep him solvent.

"I'm sorry, Colonel. It's dreadful, what's happened." He felt like saying more, even reaching to take Graves' arm or shoulder, but it seemed inappropriate.

"We all go on, you know. Life doesn't stop because you have a bit of bad luck."

Graham's eyebrows shot up of their own accord. Something about the Colonel's tone told him the older man didn't just mean Sylvia's passing. "Bad luck, Colonel?"

"Yes. Over in Miami. The buggers got a step ahead of themselves. Nobody consulted me, of course. Must think I'm bloody made of money." The anger was real, and coming so soon after the grief and sadness, it was a shock to Graham.

"Do you mind if I ask about it?" Graham deliberately pushed his notebook away a few inches, as if reassuring the Colonel that they were speaking off the record.

"There was another apartment in the same building. My investor friends saw this as an easy sell, you know. We're already marketing to the right clients, already canvassing the right neighborhoods. May as well get two sales for our efforts, right? So they quickly chucked in another seventy-five thousand dollars each. I mean, can you imagine?"

"A little rich for your blood?" Graham guessed.

"Too bloody right! They never even asked. And then they turn around and said, 'Well, if you're not interested in doubling down like this, we're not sure we can work with you.' In danger of losing my place in the group. Getting turfed out because I lacked the... Well, you know what I mean."

"I think I do. Very presumptuous of them."

"Oh, they've been doing this kind of thing for years, the bloody *sharks*. Thinning down the ranks until there's only three or four of them left to share the best leads, the best deals. They court potential investors, persuade them to join, treat them nicely, then squeeze them out when they don't show sufficient fortitude, you know, the willingness to front *serious* cash. It's a cutthroat business. Unless you're bringing millions to the table, they treat you like an amateur."

"So, where do you stand?" Graham asked.

"Up a certain navigable waterway without a certain instrument," the Colonel grimaced. "Until..." His eyes gained a curiously faraway look. "I probably shouldn't mention this, but I know I can speak in confidence."

Graham pushed his notebook another few inches away. "My lips are sealed."

Leaning in close, the Colonel delivered the news in a conspiratorial whisper. "Alice loaned me the money. All of it. Fronted me for the second apartment, helped me keep myself in the game. I showed those buggers who they're dealing with!"

"Alice Swift?" DI Graham was anxious to confirm.

"The very same. Remarkable woman. Sees the best in people, you know?"

"I'm sure," Graham replied. Inwardly, he was a blur of thought. He had so many questions, each more difficult to pose than the last. "And, if it's not too indelicate a question, what was the nature of your repayment agreement?"

"Oh, all fair and above board," he said. "I even started paying her back a little, last month, from the proceeds of a small sale up in the Florida Panhandle. Only my third effort and not a bad one," he said, rubbing his hands slightly. "But nothing on the scale of these Miami properties," he said, as if himself in awe of the risks he'd agreed to take.

Although badly distracted by this new complexity to their case, Graham kept up appearances for the remainder of their dinner. The Colonel, to Graham's relief, had no interest in dessert, as he was trying to 'keep trim.' Just after nine, Graham left Graves to enjoy an after-dinner Scotch. "I might catch up with that fellow, Alves," the Colonel told him as he was leaving. "Not much of a talker, but when he does... *fascinating* chap. Been *everywhere*."

Graham decided to sleep on the new information, rise early, and call everyone together for a morning meeting. Later, he tried to sleep, tried to let his thoughts settle on something other than the unhappy demise of Sylvia Norquist. But he was kept awake past midnight by the persistent thought that this case, frustrating and elusive by turns, was finally ready to break wide open. Something told him that tomorrow would be the day.

CHAPTER SIX

GRAHAM INITIALLY THOUGHT that bringing in a blackboard on an easel might help them brainstorm more efficiently. Seeing it now, covered in scrawled notes, scratched-out and half-deleted ideas, and a couple of hare-brained diagrams, he was beginning to wonder. They had been 'bringing together the investigative strands,' as he'd originally put it, which in reality was closer to arguing like cats and dogs, for three hours, and he was ready for a break.

"Okay, take ten, boys and girls," he said, relieved to be shooing them out of his office for a moment. "We'll all feel better after a breath of fresh air and a cuppa."

The two constables argued all the way to the front door, where they berated each other for the duration of Barnwell's cigarette. Back in his office, Graham gave Sergeant Harding a tired smile and shook his head.

"Feel as though we're getting anywhere?" he asked.

Harding took one look at the board, grabbed the eraser and cleaned the whole thing. Then she began writing in large, clear letters.

"We've got Sylvia. Late of this parish. Known to all the suspects," she says. "This fits with the very high probability that the victim knew the murderer."

"Near certainty," Graham confirmed.

"There's the exotic and charismatic Mr. Carlos Alves. Visitor from South America," she said, writing his name on the board with a dotted line to Sylvia. "Father of a teenaged boy who died while under her care."

"Bloody tragic," Graham added.

"But *not present* during the period leading up to the murder. We have confirmation of that," she said.

"From none other than the investigative powerhouse that is Constable Roach," Graham quipped.

"Marvelous. His terrifying wife is nowhere to be seen, and we have no reason to believe she's on Jersey, so the people with the most obvious motive can be ruled out."

"Ninety-nine percent," Graham confirmed. He was never happy with "always" or "absolutely." There had already been too many exceptions and rarities during his career.

"Then we have the Pilkingtons," she said, adding their names to the list. "Known to Sylvia through her work. Nigel was the recipient of successful cancer treatment, though in his unfortunate case, the Big-C appears to have returned," she said.

"Much to the shock of Mrs. Pilkington," Graham added.

"And she was just as shocked that her husband had seen Sylvia without her knowledge. And angry. Are we putting that down to... well, them just being a funny couple?"

"You tell me, Sergeant. How likely is it, all things considered, that an oncologist becomes involved with a very sick patient?"

"It must happen, but I can't think it's too frequent."

"And, not to be rude about the man, but you saw Nigel. Not exactly male model material. Am I right?"

"You are," Harding confirmed. "I mean, it wasn't as though the years were weighing heavily on Sylvia. She could have done so much better."

"Hard to say," Graham told her. "I've only ever seen her buried in a sand dune, or laid out on a mortuary slab, dead as a dodo."

Harding continued writing. "So, whatever is going on between the much troubled Pilkingtons, we can't pin a murder on them."

"Very difficult to do at present," Graham agreed. "They only have reasons to be grateful to her. And mad at each other, but that's not the point."

The board was filling with names, lines, and notes, but at least it was a more orderly depiction of the case than their previous attempt. "Okay, so we're assuming Alves didn't pay off an assassin?" Harding posited.

Graham was shaking his head. "I really can't imagine him murdering Sylvia in any other way than with his own two hands. Revenge killings are brutal. This was a quick bit of poisoning. Doesn't fit."

Sergeant Harding agreed. "And even if he had paid to have her poisoned, would he use a method like Wolfsbane?"

"More likely something which would draw out the process, not kill her in the course of an unpleasant afternoon," Graham said.

Standing back from the board, Harding said, "So, we're looking for someone else entirely."

"Yes," Graham said. He stood and began pacing around the tiny office. "Think about this," he was saying. "Why would the murderer stay around on Jersey after doing the deed?"

"If I'd just done somebody in, I'd take myself as far away as possible," Harding told him, brushing chalk off her hands.

Graham tried the opposite approach, just to play Devil's Advocate. "The murderer might have stayed in town just to deflect suspicion. As if to say, 'Look, I'm still here! I've got nothing to hide!'"

"But in that case," Harding countered, "we'd have something else on them, some connection or motive or... *something*."

Graham took the chalk. "Next. Colonel Graves."

"Our erstwhile paramour and real estate mogul," Harding quipped.

"Now, now, Sergeant," Graham said with admonishment in his tone. "He's hurting, and he's the real deal."

"You told me," Harding asserted, "that no one can be ruled out entirely."

"But how does he benefit from killing the woman he's about to propose to? If she had been the one to loan him money, I'd bite, but she was just a sweet, retired doctor. And he was crazy about her."

"That's true. Half the hotel knew about the two of them. And Mrs. Taylor, of course."

Graham stopped short. "Can we rule her out, too?"

"Oh, God, yes," Harding said at once. "Murders might boost a hotel's reputation if a celebrity is involved and a few decades go by, but all she's done since we arrived is remind us how important the summer is to her business."

"Exactly. It does her no good to have a bunch of police officers running around."

Harding thought on. "I mean, there's no way she's in a weird love triangle with Sylvia and the Colonel?"

DI Graham couldn't help a quick, indulgent laugh. "Wow, Sergeant, that's imaginative. I mean, we've got no reason to suspect it, but I like your ingenuity."

Barnwell reappeared at the door. "Oi, what the bloody hell happened to my diagram?" he demanded. "I *had* something there."

"What you *had*," Harding informed him, "was fit for a kindergarten art class. This," she announced, "is much better."

Arms folded, Barnwell took his seat and let the two continue to brainstorm. Roach slid in next to him. He turned over yet another page of his legal pad, ready to keep track of his own thoughts as he had throughout the investigation.

"What about Alice?" Harding prompted.

"She loaned Graves money," Graham told them. "It might not be in any way relevant, but I just want to put it out there."

"Money? What for?" Roach asked.

Graham explained about the Miami deal, the way that Graves was being pressured by the investment group. "He's already started paying it back," he added.

Barnwell chortled obscenely. "Paying it back *how*, exactly?"

Harding gave him yet another exasperated look, hands on her hips. "What are you talking about?"

"I mean, you saw her. That Alice, she's totty, she is." Barnwell said, narrowly preventing himself from clarifying his point with a lewd gesture. "Is it so impossible to believe?"

"That Colonel Graves was cheating on his beloved Sylvia? Or that Alice Swift, with all of her..." Harding said, barely believing she was stooping so low, "*assets*, would be interested in a sixty-year-old ex-soldier with the stiffest..."

"Steady on," Barnwell interjected.

"*Upper lip*," Harding enunciated, "you've ever seen." She rolled her eyes at Graham, as if to say, *How can I work with these buffoons?*

"Let's put a pin in that one," Graham said diplomatically. "Does Alice have any motive to harm Sylvia?" Three pairs of shoulders raised slightly, then dropped back down. "Thanks, team. Excellent police work," the DI said with heavy sarcasm.

"If there isn't anything to be found," Barnwell objected, "we aren't going to find it, are we?"

"Okay, you're right," Graham allowed. "So, who are we left with?"

"There's suicide. We haven't gone back over that," Barnwell insisted.

"Because it's bollocks," Roach countered.

"So sure?" Graham asked.

Roach was adamant. "She was happy, in love, living on the beautiful island of Jersey in the summer time, with plenty of money. What *possible reason*..."

"I don't want to give this idea more credence than I should," Graham said cautiously, "but just because someone *seems* happy doesn't necessarily mean they *are*."

"Look at Marilyn Monroe," Roach offered.

"I often do," Barnwell replied.

"Moving on," Graham decided. "If none of the hotel staff are suspects, and we can rule out everyone we've interviewed, then..."

"We're kind of nowhere," Roach said despondently.

Graham stood. "Bugger it. I'm going for a walk. If you

are struck by a bolt of investigative lightning in the next half hour, call me."

It was a bright, sunny lunchtime outside, one of the warmest days of the year so far. Graham left his jacket behind and rolled up his sleeves. It might even, he wondered to himself, be an opportunity to replace his pasty Londoner look with something a little more exotic. Not to mention *attractive.*

He walked west, on autopilot almost, toward the ocean. The cliff tops gave spectacular views of the other island beyond and then the coast of France, especially on a day as clear as this. He reached the top after twenty minutes at a meandering stroll and sat down on the grass. Quite a few years earlier, he'd been invited to a meditation retreat in Scotland that had scenery a little like this; green meadows, sparse little villages with twisting roads disappearing into the next valley, and breathtaking views of the serene, sparkling, summertime Atlantic. He'd spent a long weekend simply breathing in and out. It hadn't *really* been his thing, if he were honest. By the third day, he was bored beyond belief, but the invitation had come from a particularly alluring brunette named Isla, and he could hardly refuse, especially when she'd asked so nicely....

Without any warning whatsoever, a light bulb went off in his head. It illuminated areas of his mind, details of his memory that had languished in darkness. New connections were made, even as he sat there, stunned by the suddenness of the sensation. Pieces fell into place. The events of the last four days sought to relate to each other in novel ways and with a fresh logic.

"Bloody hell."

He stood, reaching for the notebook in his jacket pocket

before remembering that it was on the back of his office chair, at the station.

He covered the mile back to the Constabulary at a pace that would have impressed a much younger man, exhilarated by the energizing power of raw, independent discovery.

CHAPTER SEVEN

THE THREE POLICE officers stood in the lobby of Gorey Constabulary, looking at one another in confusion. Banished from DI Graham's office while he made what seemed to be a series of phone calls, they were left wondering what on *earth* he might have stumbled upon during his afternoon walk.

"You don't think," Barnwell shared in a low tone, "that our new boss is a bit loopy, do you?"

Harding gave him a skeptical look. "No, Constable. I don't."

"I mean," Barnwell pressed on, "I like a breath of fresh air as much as the next man, but..."

Graham emerged from his office, swinging back the door so hard that it smacked into the wall. "Friends, Romans, Countrymen," he began oratorically, "lend me your car so I can get over to the White House Inn and put this sodding case to bed, once and for all."

"Breakthrough, boss?" Roach asked, excited.

Graham turned to him. "Maybe. I won't know for sure until we all do a bit of people-watching. I just called Mrs.

Taylor, and she's racing around the Inn right now, doing us a favor."

The drive over was purposeful and speedy, despite the wandering tourists on this sunny afternoon. They stopped at a pedestrian crossing to allow an elderly man to cross, but he changed his mind in the middle and headed back the way he'd come. "Dozy bugger," Harding muttered. "Does he think we're in a police car because we like the colors?"

"Should have put the siren on," Barnwell recommended from the back seat. "Give him a good scare."

"Thank you, Constable," Graham said, "but I'd rather deal with Dr. Norquist's murder than a random stranger's heart attack. And buckle your seat belt. You do know the law around here, don't you?"

Mrs. Taylor was as good as her word, as always. "Good afternoon, Detective Inspector. I must say, I was surprised to receive your call, but it's good news that this might all be over soon," she enthused.

"I make no promises, Mrs. Taylor," Graham reminded her. "But I've got a hunch. And sometimes that's enough."

The Inn's staff, including the bustling and efficient Marcella, had cleared the terrace except for one large table. Around it were seated seven familiar figures. Per Graham's instructions, Carlos Alves was seated furthest from the door, followed by the Pilkingtons, Colonel Graves, and then Alice Swift. Mrs. Taylor and Marcella took the last two seats. Harding, Roach, and Barnwell positioned themselves around the terrace as Graham strode into the middle and addressed the group.

"Thank you all for being here this afternoon," he began. "I'm sure the past few days have been difficult for everyone. Sylvia was a popular and respected lady, and she will be sorely missed by many, including some of you," Graham said carefully. Not everyone on this terrace, he knew full well, was devastated at this particular loss.

"You've all been very generous with your time and for the most part," he emphasized, "entirely honest in your statements to the police." There was a flutter of concern throughout the group. Which of them was being accused of dishonesty was uncertain. "My team and I," Graham continued, motioning to the trio, "have exhausted every avenue of inquiry, including the forensic angles, and we're here today for what amounts to... Well, I suppose it's a final interview, done *en masse*," he explained. "Does anyone have any objections to this rather unorthodox format?"

No one spoke. Roach was writing, just as Graham had instructed, keeping a log, not of what was *said*, but of what each person *did*. Before being reduced to his solo evening games of solitaire, Roach had been a decent poker player and had even won a local championship. Reading people's reactions, he'd insisted to Graham on his first day in the job, was a specialty, and one which the DI was keen to put to good use.

"I'm going to lay out our case as plainly as I can," Graham said. "Nothing is for certain in this game, but we're ninety-nine percent certain that Sylvia was murdered." The Pilkingtons both gasped slightly, but that was the only movement Roach could detect. "We are also ninety-nine percent certain that she was poisoned with an herbal concoction known as 'tincture of aconite.'"

The Colonel looked thoroughly appalled. Perhaps it was guilt at the revelation of what he had done, Graham conjectured, or simply distaste at being told the very method by which his beloved had been taken from him. Alice was frowning as though puzzling the matter over in her mind. Over on Graham's left, Alves was rolling an unlit cigar between his fingers, as though supremely indifferent to this whole business.

"Aconite, or Wolfsbane as it is also known, is a deadly poison, but not an especially commonplace one. It has the virtues of being largely undetectable by pathologists as it leaves no traces of its own, save the symptoms of the poisoning itself: asphyxia caused by a dangerously irregular heart rhythm."

The Colonel was having trouble gathering his emotions. For an instant, Graham wondered whether it was a mistake inviting the man here but reminded himself that for this conjurer's trick to be a success, every participant in the investigation had to be present.

"So, once those facts were established," he told the group, "our investigation shifted its focus to potential motives. And here," he said, "we had an obvious place to begin." Graham turned to face Carlos Alves. "Sir, it is no secret that you harbored ill will toward Dr. Norquist."

Alves said nothing, continuing to roll his cigar to and fro.

"She was responsible to an extent that varies depending on who you ask for the tragic death of your son." Alves raised his eyes now and nodded slightly. "There is no greater pain in human life than such a terrible thing. But unfortunately, it made you our prime suspect."

"It would have been a pleasure," Alves said with studied malevolence, "to deny life to the woman who took my son from me."

Colonel Graves made to stand, but Barnwell responded quickest, a firm hand cautioning the incensed ex-officer to go no further.

"But I was not responsible for this crime," Alves said finally.

"No, you were not," Graham conceded. "You were on Guernsey at the time of the murder. Unless, of course," he added, "you paid someone to carry out this act."

Alves gave Graham a furious look. "*Paid?* I wouldn't pay to have such a thing done. I would have done it myself!" He paused. "But I didn't."

"No, indeed," Graham asserted. "We were discussing *motive*," he reminded the group. "Anne Pilkington. You had just such a motive, did you not?"

Her hand flew to her chest. "Me?" she gasped.

"You were concerned that your husband might be having an affair with Sylvia. You suspected that, during the course of his treatment, they had become close. Even intimate."

Nigel, for his part, looked thoroughly downcast and exhausted. Roach could only imagine that these repeated reminders of his life-and-death struggle with cancer were weighing on him. "I suspected nothing of the sort," Anne retorted. "Nigel and I are as close as we have ever been."

"But you were furious when you discovered they'd been spending time together," Graham reminded her.

Shaking her head firmly, Anne replied, "We made a pact after his diagnosis last year that we would be absolutely honest with each other. It was the first time Nigel had hidden anything from me since then."

"But for your own good," Nigel offered sincerely. "If you'd known we were meeting, you'd have known the cancer was back. And this time... Well, I couldn't put you through all that again." They sat, hand in hand, bereft. "I was going to walk out into the bay one night and never come back." The couple embraced and then sat in an intense, shared silence, seemingly no longer part of the drama unfolding around them.

Harding was close to tears, but Graham regained his focus quickly. "Which brings us to Colonel Graves." This was not, Graham could see, going to be an easy moment. "More often than you might believe," Graham said, "and far more often than any of us would like, it is those closest to the victim who are responsible for their death."

"You can't think..." Graves began, red-faced.

"I *have* to, Colonel. During investigations like this, we are obliged to ask the hardest questions and follow the most unlikely leads. You claimed to us that you were about to propose to Sylvia."

"I... I was," he replied.

"But we were forced to wonder whether you already had and had been refused. All of those carefully-laid plans ruined," Graham speculated. "Your future happiness in tatters."

Graves was silently shaking his head.

"Or perhaps you asked her for money to bail out your troubled investments in the States, and *this* was the refusal which cost Sylvia her life."

"I discussed that with you," he rasped, "in *confidence*."

"And I apologize for deceiving you. My business is catching a murderer, whatever misfortunes might have befallen yours."

"This is outrageous!" he roared. "You have *no right* to speak to me like this!"

"I have every right," Graham shot back, "to question those whom I believe may be complicit in a murder and to do so in any way I see fit."

Harding was becoming worried. Was Barnwell right, she wondered, and their new DI was a bit "loopy?" Were his methods, including this strange performance on the terrace, really sound? Were his conclusions, whatever they might be, truly to be trusted?

But before she could intervene, there was an angry voice from the next table. "You leave him *alone*!" Alice insisted. "He did *nothing* wrong."

There was silence on the terrace for a long moment. Then Graham resumed where he had left off. "Miss Swift. I wonder if there's anything you'd like to tell us?"

She sat stubbornly, her arms folded.

"Perhaps why it was that you decided to order *aconitum* flowers online?" Graham asked. "Perhaps why you chose to concoct a poison amid the dyes and inks in your room?"

Alice remained silent, staring straight ahead at the ocean.

"Perhaps why," Graham asked, approaching her now, "you added a fatal dose of Wolfsbane to Sylvia's wine while pretending to be her friend and sharing confidences?"

The first to stand was Carlos Alves, his cigar forgotten on the table, his face fixed with amazement. "Perhaps why," Graham pressed on, sensing the growing tumult among the others, "you stayed with her throughout the painful, excruciating symptoms of Wolfsbane poisoning?" Now the Colonel was up and staring at Alice. "Why you kept her from calling for help? Took her phone? Told her that everything would be fine in a moment. Even offered her more to drink, though that too was laced with the poison which was even then causing her heart to flutter and gurgle in distress?"

"My *God*..." breathed Anne Pilkington.

"Did she know what was happening in those final moments?" Graham asked Alice, the group seeming to enclose around her as though preparing to tear her apart for her sins. "Did she realize you were responsible?"

"*Her*?" Marjorie Taylor exclaimed. "But *why*?"

"This is the only thing I don't understand," Graham confessed. "Why, Alice?"

Fists clenching, jaw firmly set, Alice Swift finally spoke. "She was a temptress." Alice's voice was a furious hiss. "A *Jezebel*. A consumer of men, heedless of others and their emotions."

Alves said it for them all. "What in *God's name* is she talking about?"

The murderous woman addressed him now. "She seduced my George."

"*Your* George?" Harding said, almost unwittingly. "The Colonel, and *you*...?"

"She beguiled him. Teased him. Dangled in front of him a life so comforting and saccharine and *dull*," she spat, "and he was going to *propose*..."

"Oh, God," Colonel Graves finally managed. "Oh, Alice, what have you *done*?"

"I *had to*!" she shrieked. "There was nothing else..."

Colonel Graves spoke to Graham now, looking gaunt and ashen. "I'm sorry... I should have mentioned something about our dealings earlier... I just never, ever, in a *thousand years* would have thought..."

Without another word, Graham nodded to Sergeant Harding, who approached Alice from behind with handcuffs ready. "Alice Swift, I am arresting you on suspicion of the murder of Dr. Sylvia Norquist." As the cuffs were clicked into place, Alice seemed to struggle with inner demons known to no one else, the boiling anger and resentment that had led her to commit calculated, cold-blooded murder causing her to twitch and shudder. Harding finished reading Alice her rights and led the furious woman back from the tables toward the door where Constable

Barnwell was waiting to escort the prisoner to the police car. As Harding guided her through the doorway, Alice turned viciously and yelled at them.

"I did it for you, George!" Her voice was a cold rasp. "I *killed* her for you!"

Graves had his head in his hands, inconsolable now, as Alice was led away. "Oh, Sylvia," he said, again and again. Graham sat with the Colonel, his posture slightly slumped, relieved that his ambitious gamble had paid off and that he had successfully identified the murderer.

"It's alright, George. It's all over," he told the grieving Colonel.

"But how...?" The Colonel was plaintive.

"We now know that Miss Swift invited Dr. Norquist out for dinner the night before her body was found." DI Graham explained. "They went to the Bangkok Palace. I saw a business card for the restaurant among her weaving supplies."

"When I questioned the restaurant staff about their dinner, I learned that Alice was overheard telling Dr. Norquist about your financial woes, possibly in order to discredit you in Sylvia's eyes so that she would be persuaded not to marry you," Graham explained.

"According to staff there, the two women argued. I believe that Alice, realizing Sylvia would not renounce you, laced her drink with poison.

The Colonel shook his head and sighed deeply. He looked up at the Detective Inspector, imploring him to go on.

"Instead of taking her back to the White House Inn when she became ill," Graham continued, increasingly feeling he was intruding on the elder man's grief but also respecting his need to understand what had happened to his love, "she drove to the steps above the beach, where she plied Sylvia with more of the poisoned wine, staying with her until she was dead. I think she planned to have the tide wash Sylvia's body out to sea, but having dragged her down the steps to the beach, Alice was too exhausted to carry her further and buried her in the sand instead.

"Returning to the Inn, Swift gave herself an alibi by making sure she was seen around the hotel the following morning. She then let herself into Dr. Norquist's room, ordering her food and pretending to talk on the telephone when lunch was delivered.

"Her plan was that when the body was found, we would believe Sylvia had been alive at a time when she had, in fact, been dead for several hours. With the time of death being so vague and using a barely detectable means of killing, it would have been extremely difficult to pin the murder on Alice.

"It was a canny plan. And it nearly worked. Alice is without doubt a cold-blooded killer. You've had a lucky escape, Colonel." Graham finished quietly, knowing his words were cold comfort to the bereaved man.

The Colonel looked at the detective ruefully. "I've lost the woman I loved, my life savings, my future. I wouldn't call that much of an escape."

Graham looked down at the sad, broken man with great sympathy. He hesitated, weighing up the propriety of his action, then placed his hand on the man's shoulder.

"I'm sorry, Colonel."

As Detective Inspector Graham completed his exposition, the tension drained from the room, its occupants left to quietly contemplate the impact of his words. The room was silent and still. DI Graham delicately withdrew and as he did so, another person in the room stirred.

Stepping away from the others, and hoping not to appear indelicate, Carlos Alves quietly lit his cigar and looked out once more onto the water, a slight smile on his face for the first time in months. As he drew deeply on his cigar, he closed his eyes momentarily, and reflected on the events of the last few days. He exhaled with a small sigh, the cigar smoke dissipating into the clear Jersey air. He had all but given up. But he'd been wrong. There was an ounce of justice in the world, after all.

EPILOGUE

GOREY, THREE WEEKS LATER

SERGEANT JANICE HARDING shook her head with firm conviction. "No way, Barnwell. You've finally lost it."

"No, I'm serious," he said. "I know she's not *exactly* the right age, but there's such a thing as 'artistic license'..."

Graham emerged from his office, stretched, and regarded the squabbling pair. "What's this all about?" he asked.

Barnwell explained. "We were trying to figure out," he said, not in the least embarrassed, "who should play all of us when the Norquist case gets made into a big Hollywood movie."

"Oh, great," Graham told them. "I'm glad it's hard-nosed police work that's keeping you all so occupied."

"I thought," Barnwell continued regardless, "that Ben Affleck would make an excellent DI Graham."

"Did you, now?" Graham asked, distractedly flicking lint from his suit trousers.

"And Jodie Foster could play the fiercely devoted

Sergeant Harding," Barnwell said next. The *real* Sergeant Harding couldn't have been less impressed and made a grotesque face at the grinning Constable.

"And who's playing you, Barnwell?" Graham asked with a smirk.

"Cruise." He looked at them both. "I mean, *obviously*."

"Obviously," parroted Harding, and followed Graham back into his office.

Graham smiled at her. "Good to see him applying that investigative acumen," he quipped.

"I'd rather that than him showing up half-drunk," she said. "Don't think he's touched a drop since the case."

"Good," Graham nodded. "About time for lunch, isn't it, Sergeant?"

Harding checked the big wall clock. "I'd say so, sir."

"Well, I think it's my turn to buy. Bangkok Palace?" he recommended.

Harding grinned. "Sure. Sounds good."

Graham followed Harding out into the lobby, where Roach was now fully involved in the Hollywood discussion. "Cruise, he says," Roach was laughing. "Can you imagine?"

"Not even a little bit," Harding said, pushing open the door. "Hold the fort, you two," she instructed.

"Will do, Sarge," they chorused.

"You know," Janice said, as she got in Graham's car, "those two are in grave danger of becoming actual *police officers* one of these days." She chuckled, but not dismissively. Her own respect for Roach and Barnwell was on the rise. Ever since their new boss had arrived on Jersey, they had been punctual and diligent, keen to help the public and willing to leave no stone unturned. *I barely recognize them*, she mused to herself. "Well, DI Graham, a great detective needs a great support team."

Graham rolled his eyes. "Steady on, Sergeant." He put the car into gear with a self-contented smile, and they headed off into Jersey's bright, afternoon sunshine.

To get your free copy of *The Case of the Screaming Beauty,* the prequel to the Inspector David Graham series, plus two more books, updates about new releases, exclusive promotions, and other insider information, sign up for Alison's mailing list at:

https://www.alisongolden.com/graham

INSPECTOR DAVID GRAHAM WILL RETURN…

WOULD YOU LIKE to find out how life on Jersey continues to suit Inspector Graham as he settles in? Find out in the next book in the Inspector Graham cozy mystery series, *The Case of the Fallen Hero*. You'll find an excerpt on the following pages.

THE CASE OF THE FALLEN HERO

PROLOGUE

Saturday, 3:30pm

THE FOUR FRIENDS tumbled out of the minivan, thanked their driver, and stared agog at the imposing medieval castle that now towered over them.

"Bloody hell," Harry managed, wiping his glasses clean and staring at the huge walls. "It's *big*, isn't it?"

Emily retrieved her priceless violin from the van's back seat and joined him, looking up at the impenetrable, solid battlements that spoke of the castle's impressively deep history. "Going for your Masters in architecture, then, Harry?" she joked. "It's an eight hundred-year-old *fortress*. I don't think *big* does it justice."

Harry made sure his battered cello case had suffered no further indignities on the ferry ride over from Weymouth and hoisted its weight onto his shoulder with well-practiced ease. "Well, I wouldn't dream of upstaging our resident expert, you see."

Leo Turner-Price, accomplished historian and violinist,

stared at the castle as though achieving a lifelong dream. "Emily is right about the structure being eight *hundred* years old. But there are records of substantial fortifications on this site that go back to the Bronze Age."

"Really?" Harry remarked. "Wow."

"All to keep out the beastly French," Marina observed. The youngest of the four members of the Spire String Quartet, Marina was a shy but – as Harry once described her in an unguarded moment – "insanely attractive" viola player who taught young children at two of London's most expensive schools. "Must have cost a fortune."

"Well, if that was their aim," Harry opined, keeping up his role as the "bluff Brit abroad," "it was money well spent."

Emily rolled her eyes. Fifteen years into her friendship with the wonderfully gruff, plentifully bearded Harry Tringham, she found that he was still learning how to filter the thoughts that entered his overactive brain, far too many of which were given unwisely free passage direct to his equally active mouth. She spotted the visitors' entrance up some steps in front of them. "Shall we?"

Emily was, in fact, the only member of the quartet to have visited Orgueil Castle before, or even to have performed on the island of Jersey. It was through her contact with the castle's highly professional events manager, Stephen Jeffries, that they had been booked for the evening's wedding festivities. Always in need of a dependable ensemble who could provide light background music one moment and a strident processional the next, Jeffries kept Emily's name at the top of his hiring list. He had been heartily impressed when, during a wedding two years before, Emily had led a young string trio through various weather-related disasters, a collapsed marquee, and a bridal arrival so delayed that the groom was harboring the gravest of doubts, all before dashing off a beautifully polished *Prince of Denmark's March* as the sodden bride entered, still dripping, into the Great Hall.

"Emily, my *darling*!" Jeffries exclaimed as he walked out to greet them. "*So* lovely to see you! How's your teaching going? Didn't you just start at that exclusive little prep school?" he asked.

"Fine, fine," Emily told him. "It's going well. Some of the little blighters even manage to practice before their lessons." The whole quartet was nodding. Finding students who were prepared to work hard was like finding gemstones in the desert. "It's nice to get a break, though, and a change of scenery."

"Better weather for this one, too, eh?" Jeffries said, hand aloft toward the bluest possible sky.

"Much better," Emily agreed. "And I want to thank you for this, Stephen. Gives us all a nice break from an unseasonably warm London. This is Marina Linton," she said as the tall blonde extended a graceful hand, "Harry Tringham, our cellist and resident physicist," she added, "and the historian Leo Turner-Price."

"Simply delighted to be here," Leo enthused. "Remarkable building, really."

Jeffries led them into an open quadrangle that was home to a beautifully kept maze and then down some steps into the castle's administrative area. Here they would relax and tune up until the wedding guests began to arrive at five o'clock. He moved paperwork and wedding paraphernalia off his biggest table to give them a safe, flat surface for their priceless instruments.

"Okay, did everyone's folders survive the journey?" Emily wanted to confirm and received a trio of nods in reply. "Excellent," she said, quickly tying her curly, black hair into an unsophisticated ponytail. "So, we'll start with the little Baroque set..."

"Couperin," Harry said, finding the sheet music in his folder.

"And then the Purcell theater music?" Marina asked.

"That's right. Then *Eine Kleine.* Everyone loves that," Emily continued.

"All four movements?" Leo asked.

Emily thought for a second. "Let's play it by ear. Depends on timings and such, but we can axe the repeats if we need to hurry things along."

"Righto," Leo said, slotting the pages in the correct order. "Which Processional did they choose in the end?"

Marina clasped both hands together, as if in prayer. "*Please* tell me it isn't Wagner again. I promised I'd quit weddings if I ever had to..."

"Nope," Emily reassured her. "*The Arrival of the Queen of Sheba.*"

All four sighed slightly. "It's a terrific piece," Leo allowed, "but too much of a gallop for a processional, surely?"

Emily found the music and finished organizing her own folder. "She's the bride, Leo. And it's her..."

"*Special day!*" the quartet chorused and then laughed together.

Jeffries watched this polished routine with unconcealed envy. "Honestly," he said as the four musicians finalized their folders, "I would simply *die* to make every aspect of these weddings as smooth as working with you guys."

"Aw, Stephen. You're an angel," Emily replied, giving him a kiss on the cheek.

"I've already had a run-in with the mother of the bride," he admitted, his face relating just how ugly the encounter had been. "*Terrifying* woman. A foot wider than I am," he confessed, "and with a decidedly mean streak. These people get it into their heads that just because they've spent a fortune on getting their offspring hitched, they can treat people *however they like*!"

Jeffries was a stylish and experienced man, unused to brusque treatment. He allowed that the bridal party was under considerable pressure to ensure their lovely daughter's wedding day was as close to perfect as possible, but still, their discourtesy toward him seemed so unnecessary, especially when he was doing his level best to meet their every need.

"I'll leave you to it. Yell if you need anything," Stephen said with a companionable hand on Emily's forearm, and then, with a dramatic flourish, he left to supervise the preparation of the reception.

Emily's preference was to begin playing even before the guests arrived, ostensibly to create the "right atmosphere," but more practically to check acoustics and intonation. The quartet seated themselves in the corner of the quadrangle where the marquee – the same one that had suffered the spectacular structural failure during Emily's last performance at the castle – was set up. Guests would shortly be wandering on the lawn of the quad, ducking inside to grab a drink or a canapé, and generally rubbing shoulders before the arrival of the bridal party.

The group went through the plan, talking quietly in the short gaps between movements of the tasteful Couperin suite Harry had arranged for them years before. Once it was confirmed that the bride was ready to go through with the ceremony (and in Emily's twenty-year experience of weddings, this was by no means an absolute certainty), the quartet would have only a few moments to quickly relocate to the Great Hall and prepare for the Processional.

Later, after the bride reached the altar, the musicians' time would be their own. Jeffries would hand them a generous check each, and they'd enjoy the rest of the evening at the castle before retreating to a local hostel for the night. The castle, for its part, would then play host to an extended party before the guests collapsed into bed; there was plentiful accommodation within the giant edifice so that, as Jeffries always thought of it, they wouldn't have to stagger far.

"Let's skip the minor-key Purcell movements," Marina advised. "I don't feel like playing in D-minor under a sky as beautiful as this." The quartet unanimously agreed and launched into the joyously dotted rhythms of Purcell's more animated theater pieces. The eighty or so invitees were arriving in a steady stream, and the quadrangle filled with music, the clink of wine glasses, and old friends catching up after too long apart.

Their intonation unimprovable and their balance as tightly controlled as ever, the quartet quietly reveled in the freedom of simply playing for fun. After the second movement of *Eine Kleine Nachtmusik,* Harry leaned over to Marina and grinned. "Doesn't really feel like work, does it?"

"Not even a little bit," she said, following Emily's lead for the beginning of the *Minuet.*

An excitable Stephen Jeffries scuttled over. "She's *here*!" he announced in a boisterous whisper. "Action stations!"

Emily used eye contact alone – as the best leaders can –

to bring the Minuet to a quick but elegant halt, and the quartet made their way to the Great Hall, slightly in advance of the politely ushered guests. Moments later, the ravishing Marie Joubert – soon to be Marie Ross –stepped steadily and confidently down the aisle in her white lace gown with its elaborate train, the filigree of Handel and the beaming smiles of her family her lasting accompaniment.

To get your copy of The Case of the Fallen Hero, visit the link below:
https://www.alisongolden.com/fallen-hero

BOOKS BY ALISON GOLDEN

FEATURING REVEREND ANNABELLE DIXON

Death at the Café (Prequel)

Murder at the Mansion

Body in the Woods

Grave in the Garage

Horror in the Highlands

Killer at the Cult

FEATURING DIANA HUNTER

Hunted (Prequel)

Snatched

Stolen

Chopped

Exposed

ABOUT THE AUTHOR

Alison Golden is the *USA Today* bestselling author of the Inspector David Graham mysteries and Reverend Annabelle Dixon cozy mysteries. As A.J. Golden, she writes the Diana Hunter thriller series.

Alison was raised in Bedfordshire, England. Her aim is to write stories that are designed to entertain, amuse, and calm. Her approach is to combine creative ideas with excellent writing and edit, edit, edit.

Alison is based in the San Francisco Bay Area with her husband and twin sons. She splits her time between London and San Francisco.

For up-to-date promotions and release dates of upcoming books, sign up for the latest news here: https://www.alisongolden.com/graham.

For more information:
www.alisongolden.com
alison@alisongolden.com

facebook.com/alisongolden.books
twitter.com/alisonjgolden
instagram.com/alisonjgolden

THANK YOU

Thank you for taking the time to read *The Case of the Hidden Flame*. If you enjoyed it, please consider telling your friends or posting a short review. Word of mouth is an author's best friend and very much appreciated.

Thank you,

Alison

Made in the USA
Monee, IL
27 February 2020